THE HUNGRY WALK

BY

SONIA KELLY

authorHOUSE™

1663 LIBERTY DRIVE, SUITE 200
BLOOMINGTON, INDIANA 47403
(800) 839-8640
WWW.AUTHORHOUSE.COM

AuthorHouse™
1663 Liberty Drive, Suite 200
Bloomington, IN 47403
www.authorhouse.com
Phone: 1-800-839-8640

AuthorHouse™ UK Ltd.
500 Avebury Boulevard
Central Milton Keynes, MK9 2BE
www.authorhouse.co.uk
Phone: 08001974150

First published by AuthorHouse   6/5/2006

ISBN: 1-4208-9146-4 (sc)

*Printed in the United States of America
Bloomington, Indiana*

This book is printed on acid-free paper.

TABLE OF CONTENTS

THE HUNGRY WALK

"Go to God, Micheáleen", muttered the woman as with failing strength she consigned the body of her young brother to the turbulent waters of Killary Bay, as they sucked greedily at the base of the cliff.

The year was 1847 and Ellen Clancy had already disposed of the bodies of her parents and two sisters in a similar fashion. There was nothing left for her now but to make for the workhouse in the town of Westport, some twenty miles to the north.

She returned to the cabin where they had lived, drained of sorrow, and almost drained of hope, despair and hunger having etched their story on her face. She appeared more like a woman of fifty than one of twenty-five.

Now she covered her once-bright hair with an old black shawl, gathered the rest of her tattered rags around her and stepped out barefooted along the track that led away from home. She had eaten nothing for two days - the last of the oatmeal had made a gruel for Micheal the previous night, but by morning the life had left him, too, and she was all alone.

The morning was still young when she set off, the way winding at first around the convoluted shores of the bay, then striking out across the intervening lowland. She stumbled on, her mind numbed with misery, her feet soon swollen and blistered.

There were eight miles behind her and her footsteps were faltering when a river touched the track on its way from the distant hills to the bay. The temptation to bathe her aching feet in its dark ripples was irresistible and she climbed down the bank to sit where she could dangle them in the water.

The coolness brought her some relief and after a while she withdrew them, drying them on the ends of her ragged skirt. But her strength had ebbed away with the flowing river and when she regained the track, she found she could go no further. She lay down on the grass and closed her eyes and waited for some energy to return to her.

None did. Even the will to move forward left her and she drifted off into a state of semi-consciousness.

It was towards evening when a man came walking down from the hills along the riverbank. From high up where he had been tending his sheep, he had watched the progress of the walker and had seen where she had come to rest. He had noted the now seemingly lifeless position of her body.

He himself was strong and full of energy, and why would he not be, for there were plenty of salmon in the river up in the remote fastness of the glen, which was his home, and the landlord's agent was a poor reckoner of his master's sheep, never daring to stay long enough in the threatening hills to make a full check. For four generations the Cochrans had been shepherds and they were, to some extent, masters of their own patch.

Now Tomas, the eldest son, lent over the prostrate figure and saw that she was still breathing. He shook her gently.

She opened her eyes to see a tall man in rough clothes, with a cap over his dark hair and a stick in his hand looming above her. With a gasp she struggled to sit up. "Westport", she murmured faintly. "I'm for the workhouse, but…" and hopeless tears began to course down her cheeks.

"That's a sorry place to be heading", he answered her. "And the way you look to me, you'll not be getting there!"

"I have to - there's naught else." Her voice was barely audible, swamped by tears.

"You'll come with me," the shepherd said. Without further delay he slid an arm beneath her body and heaved her onto his shoulder. Then, her bare feet pressed into his gansy in front and her disheveled hair tumbling down his back, he set off with great strides up along the river's course towards unknown country.

Ellen made no resistance. Indeed, she was scarcely capable of doing so. She knew that her journey would have ended by the side of the track if this wild man had not appeared so, wherever they were bound for, it might be better - there might be food - she let her mind drift around this almost unimaginable possibility as she continued to lie limply like a sack slung across a bank.

The land began to rise and the sound of the river changed as rocks impeded its flow, but the pace of the climber barely lessened and the hungry track seemed far below when the terrain leveled out and beneath her drooping head she saw crude wooden planks and knew they were crossing a river. A few more steps and they were passing over the threshold of a dwelling.

Then she was being lowered onto a chair and her rescuer was saying, "The colleen is famished. It's near death she was when I saw her."

"The Lord save us, Tomas!"

Having lowered his burden, Tomas stepped back and the room came into view. It was small and low ceilinged, with a flagged floor and a big open fireplace. On each side of it sat an old man and an old woman. It was the latter who had spoken in response to the explanation. She now got up and took the lid off a black pot that stood at the side of the glowing turf and began to ladle some of its contents into a bowl. She handed it to Ellen, together with a spoon. "It's welcome you are," she said. "Let you take this sup to refresh you."

Ellen thought she would faint from the wonderful fragrance of the broth. She could hardly murmur her thanks before the spoon was to her lips and the flavours of mountain lamb and herbs and barley like she had never tasted before were caressing her tongue. Ahh... with each swallow she felt the strength returning to her limbs. Finally she put the bowl down on the table beside her and looked up at Tomas, who had moved to the other side of the table and now leant against a well-furnished dresser. "You saved my life", she said. "Now tomorrow I can continue on."

A faint smile lightened his dark features, but he said nothing. It was his father who responded. The old man, silent until now, pushed back his cap, then held out his hand to her. "Let there be no rush on you, lass," he said, "you're welcome here to the home of Rory Cochran. Pull up to the fire now and tell us what misfortune is on you."

She obeyed, while Tomas dipped into the pot and extracted his own supper. "I'm Ellen Clancy," she told them, "from beyond Leenane. The hunger took my family - every one of them, the last this morning. I'm heading for the workhouse."

"Aye," said the old man, "we heard the situation was awful bad. Up here it doesn't bother us - we have plenty always."

They chatted on, the darkness of the night dissipated by rush lights, until Ellen's eyelids were drooping. Finally the old woman stood up. "You'll take the room below", she said, and led the way into it and to a big double bed with a feather mattress. Too tired to protest, too happy to be off the road, Ellen collapsed into the comforting softness, pulled up the quilt and was asleep before thoughts of tomorrow could bring renewed anguish.

Come morning, she awoke to sounds of the fire being prodded into life. Gathering her rags about her, she swung her legs down, but winced as her feet touched the floor. Looking at them, she saw with dismay that they were scratched and bruised and still swollen, but none the less, she limped into the kitchen. Hearing her, Tomas got up from the fire and came over. "They don't look too good," he remarked, following her gaze. "Mam will dress them for you - they'll heal in a few days."

"A few days!" Ellen was shocked. "But I must be going…"

"You'll go nowhere like that, girl." Tomas' mother had come up behind them and she, too, was bending over to examine the feet. "It's rest you need". Muttering to herself, she started taking mugs and plates down from the dresser and filling a big black kettle from a pail inside the door.

Accepting the inevitable, and not without relief, Ellen hobbled outside and surveyed the territory. High mountains enclosed a wide, level glen, with the river running a hundred yards from the thatched, white-washed cottage. A row of sheds extended from one gable, in one of which a cow was softly lowing; hens were scratching beside a stack of turf and in the distance a horse was chomping along the riverbank. Ellen wondered was she dreaming. Were there really people living like this, while famine stalked the land below?

It was no dream. Tomas emerged from one of the sheds carrying a bowl of eggs and pail of milk. "This is Glenfraugh." he told her in passing, "home to the Cochrans for two hundred years." Lost in the wonder of it, dream or not, she pottered around, attended closely by the two sheep dogs. Bran and Fionn, until called inside. On the table were the eggs fresh-boiled, a lump of golden butter and a big slab of soda bread. There was also a pot of tea, though tea was "a scarce item these days", as old Rory informed her. To Ellen it constituted a banquet, the likes of which she had not thought to see again.

When they had eaten, Tomas went off to tend the sheep and Sarah, as Ellen now knew was his mother's name, produced a basin, filled it with warm water, added some unfamiliar leaves and bade her steep her feet. After a while she lifted them out onto her lap and rubbed them with a thick, yellow grease. "Goose grease", she was told. They felt so good after the treatment that she felt she could continue on her way there and then. But Sarah had different ideas. It was the day for churning and Ellen watched as the big wooden vessel had milk poured into it and the plunger inserted. "Take a hand at this now," said Sarah, and Ellen gladly complied.

While she moved the plunger steadily up and down, Sarah talked. She told of the two daughters and the other son who had married and gone off to new homes. "We're that far from anywhere here," she explained, "they'd never be wed only for the matchmaker. It's real hard on Tomas, for there's few girls would settle in here and he cannot leave the place himself and go off. We have hopes, though," she continued. "Will Buckley said he heard tell of a girl beyond in Louisburgh who might be willing. We expect him daily." Ellen pondered on this news. She would need to be well gone to make room for this new arrival. It wouldn't do to hinder whatever remote chance Tomas had of finding a bride.

After a while the butter formed and she gathered it up and washed and salted it, while the other woman readied the midday meal. And what a meal it was - poached salmon with carrots from the garden, all laced with the newly-made butter and washed down with the fresh butter milk. They ate like kings up here, she thought. The isolation made that possible.

Later she asked for hot water and a basin. "It's time to clean up," she said. "I'm a horrible sight."

"Wait yet." Sara rummaged in a press and brought out a red flannel petticoat and a white blouse. "Put these on you - I'll not be wearing them again."

Thankfully Ellen took the clothes. She discarded her rags, had a good scrub down in the room and washed her tangled hair. She emerged a different person, the gaunt features lit by sea-green eyes that shone out from beneath a cloud of russet hair and a figure that showed every promise of voluptuous curves. "By God!" said old Rory. "Ye're a sight for sore eyes and no mistake!" Even Tomas' dark visage seemed to soften when he came in for the evening meal of broth.

The next day brought a further softening. Instead of taking to the hills with the dogs, he went into and remained in one of the sheds for a couple of hours. When he came back to the house, he carried a pair of sheepskin slippers, which he presented to Ellen. "They'll save your feet until they heal," he said awkwardly. "I just cobbled them together from an old skin."

She was delighted and put them on at once. They enabled her to move around outside and she busied herself over the next few days with whatever tasks came up. There was no further mention of Will Buckley, but she could not forget the threat of the matchmaker's impending visit and was glad when her feet were no longer sore, so that there would be no hindrance to her departure if and when it became necessary.

It was a week later when the two dogs started barking in mid-morning. Ellen had been picking carrots in the plot at the back of the cottage when she heard them. She ran to the enclosing wall from where she could see a small, hunched figure climbing up the stony path. It did not need Sarah's call of welcome to tell her that Will Buckley had come.

Determined that her hosts would find no impediment to the forthcoming match, she knew that the time had come to leave. Fortunately, she thought, she wore her own clothes, now washed and patched, and her feet were healed, so the sheepskin slippers were inside. She started down the hill, knowing that all attention would be on the visitor.

As fast as she could she covered the ground and she was a strong woman, now that vigour had returned to her limbs. The miles fell away behind her, once she was back on the north-bound track to Westport. She had reached Bohea and was thinking about finding shelter for the night, when she heard a shout behind her.

Startled, she turned, to see the amazing sight of Tomas, astride his mare and whipping her on with the rope-end of the bridle. Stopped in her tracks, half-paralysed between fear and astonishment, she waited for him to reach her.

Coming up, he slid from the horse and confronted her. "Isn't it a strange thing, now, for you to be making off," he said grimly, "when we thought you were content to be safe in the hills?"

"But the matchmaker - he brought tidings of a woman for you. I thought it was best to be going - to make room…" Her voice faltered as he started at her.

"Will Buckley has no woman for me," Tomas replied. "And I want no woman but the one I found lying near dead by the river and who brought the light of Heaven with her into the dark glen!"

The next moment she was in his arms and the shadows of night had begun to fall when he let her go. Then, gathering up the horse's reins, he swung her onto its back; with a leap, he was up behind her, urging the animal on.

Soon the drumming hooves of the mare were the only sound in the valley, as she galloped back towards the darkening hills.

THE HORSE WHISPERER

———

THE LIGHT-FOOTED STEP OF YOUNG JAMIE NOONE, AS
HE RAN ALONG THE GRASSY PATH TO THE FOOT OF THE
MOUNTAIN, WAS SEEMINGLY AT ODDS WITH THE HEAVINESS
OF HIS HEART.

He was bound for the white strand, where the annual
race meeting took place, his eager anticipation punctuated by
thoughts of the famine ship on which the Noones would be
embarking in week's time. He knew that city life was not for
him, because without the animals he grew up with, he would
be miserable.

Beneath his breath he cursed Squire Vernon, who was said
to have paid the emigrants' passage in order to free the land
for his sheep.

It was something that this, his last race meeting, promised
such sport. It seemed that Squire Vernon had wagered his black
stallion against a horse of his neighbour's and there were wild
rumours that he had staked half his property on a win. Serve
him right, thought Jamie, if the stallion loses. He hoped it
would.

He ran lightly up the shallow incline and saw that a birch tree had fallen across the path some way ahead and below. A commotion the other side was causing the branches to flail wildly. At the same moment a shrill whinny pierced the air. Then another and another.

Jamie quickened his pace and raced towards the fallen tree. Through the branch he could see a big, black horse rearing and plunging, the reins of the bridle caught around a jagged fork. "

"Woah, boy, woah", he cajoled, as he clambered towards the struggling animal.

At the sound of his voice the horse quietened and he was able to lay a hand on its head and whisper into its ear. Suddenly, docile as a child, it allowed the boy to disentangle the reins and lead it away from the branches.

But then, with a violent snort, it lashed out with a hind leg, narrowly missing it's rescuer. "Steady, steady", Jamie soothed. He sensed something was wrong and saw that the horse was reluctant to put any weight on that foot. Crooning in a language known only to himself and the animal, he lifted the hoof and examined the bottom.

SPLINTER

Sure enough, he spotted the end of a splinter protruding from beneath the shoe. Cupping the hoof with both hands, he bent his head and gripped the fragment with his teeth. A quick jerk and out came a sliver of wood. He dropped the hoof and the horse put weight on it again.

The horse danced a few steps and Jamie laughed. "Did you come from the races", he asked. "Maybe so. And it's to find your owner we should be going". He jumped up on the horse's back and they went blithely along the track, which soon joined the beach road to pass in proximity to the boundary wall of the Vernon estate.

They were approaching the back entrance of the property when Jamie espied half a dozen people running along the road towards them. They all began shouting when they saw him. The leading man came up and grabbed the bridle. "Thanks be to God", he gasped. "We thought we'd lost the Master's horse and him due to be racing within the hour".

The others drew up, all chattering at once, excitedly. "But who's to ride him, now"? The voice of one rose above the others. "And the jockey lying unconscious after a kick from himself….."

Silence descended on the whole group. Then the first man spoke. "Let the rider that's on him carry on. If he was fit to catch and tame him, He's surely fit to race".

"But the saddle"? said another. "We have no time to go for it". Jamie had never ridden with a saddle in his life. He sat on the horse bemused. It seemed he was riding the squire's famous black stallion and now he was expected to race it! Then, why not? he thought. My last race meeting will surely be one to remember. "I need no saddle", he said. "Let's go".

And so they did. The stable hands running alongside Jamie and his mount, telling him the race had to be won, or the master ruined and all of them along with him.

It was no small responsibility for a fourteen-year-old boy. Now he was supposed to win a race that he had previously hoped would be lost by this same horse. He shook his head at the wonder of it, his dark curls flying around his face.

The stallion jogged on and soon the strand was in view. The scene was thronged and all heads turned as the little group approached. Exclamations of surprise could be heard at the horse's unfamiliar rider and the lack of a saddle. "will you look at young Noone! What's he at, above on Black Peril"? "Where's the rightful jockey, at all'? "Sure, that combination will be no match for Morning Glory"?

Just then two motor cars drove up and stopped at the fringe of the crowd. Out stepped the rival owners and scanned the scene for their horses. As soon as Squire Vernon spotted his stallion, he hurried over. "What's this"? he demanded, staring at Jamie. "Where is O'Connor? Why is the horse not saddled and ready"?

SQUIRE

"My God"! The squire said, his hand up over his eyes. "All is lost", he moaned. "We have no chance now against the chestnut".

The bookmakers seemed to echo his opinion, as they shouted out the starting prices. "Ten to one Black Peril. Even money Morning Glory".

Jamie whispered incomprehensible instructions into Black Peril's ear and the horse whinnied and pawed the ground. The crowd parted and the groom led him forward to stand beside the sleek-looking chestnut that was his opponent. He snorted in disdain.

And off they went.

The course was a good two miles along the strand, around a flag pole and back to finish at the starting point. Jamie lay along the stallion's neck, his ragged trousers and bare feet in contrast to the other immaculately turned out rider that might have been degrading, were it not for the fact that he seemed to be part of his mount, sinuously flowing with the rippling muscles beneath him, black hair blending with black mane. It was a powerful and beautiful sight.

The other rider used his whip and reached the flag pole a good two lengths ahead of Black Peril. A half mile from the finish and the lead had been reduced to a length. But the squire's rival sensed victory and the crowd was shouting for Morning Glory- except for the squire's immediate retainers, who had bucked the odds and opted for the master's horse. They were now beginning to turn away, when Jamie raised his head and shouted - what words no one could say- but, as though the stallion had been stung, he leaped forward, overtaking Morning Glory in a half dozen strides, to flash past the winning post, himself a length in front.

An eerie silence engulfed the crowd. Then a wild hullabaloo broke forth in the Vernon camp. Hats were thrown in the air, Jamie was pulled from the horse and hugged, the squire was shaking his hand and telling him to come up to the Manor and the losers were muttering that it was illegal to ride the race bareback- although everyone knew that no such ruling existed.

As for Jamie. He knew now for sure that his last race meeting on the white strand would stay in his memory for ever, come what may in a distant foreign city.

Later on, back at the Manor, Squire Vernon was saying to his farm manager, "See to it that no one but the Noone boy rides Black Peril in the future".

"That may be difficult, Sir", replied the man. "The family is due to emigrate next week, according to your orders".

Colour suffused Squire Vernon's face. "They'll do no such thing"! he roared. "A boy like that is worth his weight in gold. "Have accommodation at the stables prepared for them immediately and see that the boy is dressed in a manner befitting his future responsibilities. His wages will be determined later".

"Yes, Sir". The man left to carry out his instructions, so that foreign cities were to be deprived of the Connacht Horse Whisperer, who went on to become a famous jockey that no other rider was able to beat.

THE DAY OF RECKONING

It was the Thursday before Christmas sixty years ago, the day of the Maragadh Mor - a day that was normally the highlight of the year for the country folk of west Mayo.

But for Winnie Malone it was the day of reckoning. The year had started badly with five or six pullets being killed, then a long spell of rain had delayed the spring planting and had no doubt contributed to the sickness that had carried away her brother, Packie.

Left on her own to manage the few acres as best she could, Winnie was hard put to save the customary part of all produce for the Christmas market she now faced into.

Indeed, she did not expect that the few geese she had, along with some butter and eggs and the half dozen pairs of thick-knitted socks would pay what she owed the shopkeeper in the market town. For the Maragais Mor was the time to settle debts and to pay the dues which had accumulated over the year when few people had money in hand.

SHOPKEEPER

Normally the shopkeeper in his turn would present his customers with a Christmas box. This always contained a barm brack, as well as packets of sugar, tea, raisins and whatever other items he might be inspired to add. Winnie had no expectations of receiving such a gift.

In fact, she had no idea what the outcome would be when she failed to settle the reckoning. One thing was sure - she would be without the basic items that constituted Christmas. However, as the night sky was paling, she continued to load up the ass, packing such produce as she had into the panniers that hung on each side of the animal - which looked like a strange ghost in the half-light, she thought, for it was neither white nor brown, but a patchy mixture of both as though nature had made a mistake. It was strong enough, though, and when all was packed, Winnie pulled her shawl up over her dark curls, closed the door of the cottage and the two of them set off, the frost crunching beneath their feet.

They were not the only travelers; once they reached the main route, they became part of a steady stream of carts and donkeys and people on foot, all bound for the market and looking forward to a day spent in renewing friendships, exchanging gossip and buying in the Christmas.

Winnie could not reciprocate or respond to the banter. Worry for the future enveloped her like a black cloud and she faced into the six mile journey with trepidation. She remembered the excitement of Christmas when she and Packie had been children and the return of their parents from town, the unloading of the goodies from the cart and a certain air of secrecy as some parcels were stowed away on top of the dresser, unopened.

Christmas Eve was the start of the festivities. Tea time that night was almost as important as dinner the next day. The whole family would gather and the barm brack would be cut, as well as the special currant cake and apple cake made in the house. Meat did not figure at this meal, but the adults would partake later of some of the "hard stuff". That night candles would be lit in all the windows and the next morning Santa Clause would have left Christmas stockings for the children. These were among the few things to come ready packaged. They were made of white net and filled with inexpensive sweets and baubles.

Mass on Christmas morning was at 7:30 and Winnie remembered when the four of them would leave the house and walk along the frosty road with the stars still shining overhead until the church came into view, all lit up, with the lights sparkling off the ice. Home afterwards to cook the goose in the pot oven, along with the bacon, and then the playing of Christmas games and more whisky for the adults.

Winnie sighed at the memory of good times past as she plodded on towards the town, her hand on the neck of the odd-coloured donkey.

The sun, such as it was, was well up when they reached the thronged market place. Winnie edged through the crowds until she found a space beside the weighbridge and started calling out her wares. "Eggs by the dozen, butter, fat geese, the best home-knitted socks…" Before long, all that remained in the panniers was one goose and a pair of socks. The money felt heavy in the pocket of her skirt, but when she counted it, it was £4 short of what she guessed the reckoning to be. Despair overwhelmed her and fear too of what action the shopkeeper might take.

Just then a shout arose and all heads turned to see a somewhat wild looking fellow, clearing the way with a stick and dragging an ass behind him. "By the Holy Saints of Ireland!" he was crying. "I've found the treasure at the end of the rainbow!"

Bursting through the remainder of the people around her, the stranger threw his arms around her astonished donkey and kissed it soundly on its pale muzzle.

"Haven't I travelled the length and breadth of Ireland to find this darling beast?" he enquired of his bemused audience. "With himself here," he said, jerking forward his own similar patchwork animal. "near in despair for a mate... it is a she-ass no doubt?"

He paused for an anxious moment, peering at Winnie's donkey and then seemed, for the first time, to notice its owner. He doffed his green felt hat, exposing a riot of jet black curly hair, and gave her a courtly bow. "My name is Marty Doolin," he said. "We're well met on this auspicious day."

Winnie was speechless. What was he on about - was he entirely mad? She took in his eager face and dark eyes, sparkling with excitement his baineen jersey over striped trousers and then her glance roamed over the contents of the donkey's panniers. They contained tin cans and kettles, mugs and buckets. He was a tinsmith. Such travelers were always welcome in the countryside and so she smiled at him.

"I am Winnie Malone," she said at last, "and it's the strange fuss you are making over my misbegotten ass."

PIEBALD

"Oh girl dear," the tinsmith replied. "There's a man up north would pay gold and silver for piebald asses - they're mad for them abroad in England as pets. Let us celebrate the day that's in it," he continued. "Have you a home to go to where we can dance and make merry?" And he began to dance a jig there in front of her. The people around applauded and murmured among themselves about the piebald donkeys - "did you ever hear the like of that?" and "an ass to be valuable"! They clapped and laughed.

His performance finished, Marty Doolin grasped the girl's arm. "Let us buy the makings of a feast," he said, "for this meeting calls for great celebration."

"Well, I have one goose left." she said hesitantly, not knowing how to proceed.

The traveller unclasped a leather bag from his waist and handed it to her. It was heavy with coins. "Let you go into that shop and buy what is needed for a night of revelry." he said. "I'll mind these beauties while you're gone." He then fell to crooning to the two animals, who seemed to have got acquainted themselves and had started to nuzzle each other.

DREAMING

Winnie thought she must be dreaming, as she went into the grocer's shop clasping the bag of money. "Will you let me have the reckoning, please?" she asked the elderly proprietor who looked as disbelieving as herself at the request. He had long given up hope of her being able to settle the bill. However, he totted it up and presented the total.

She emptied her own pocket and extracted the deficit from the traveller's bag. The grocer wrote out a receipt. "You'll not go without your Christmas box," he said and began packing up a selection of items.

"I'm thankful to you," Winnie told him. "You might add a bottle of whisky to the things," she said, "and two pounds of bacon and this and this and this…" She moved around the shop selecting her purchases, while the grocer watched with ever-widening eyes.

"You've come into a bit of luck, then?" He could no longer contain his curiosity. "Someone left you an inheritance?"

Winnie laughed as she paid for the extra purchases and got her arms around the big box. "It was an inheritance, surely," she said, "but it's only now I know the worth of it."

She was laughing still as she carried her purchases back to the man and the donkeys - a girl with a light step and joy in her face who had regained her childhood on one winter's afternoon.

They packed the shopping into the panniers and together they took the long road home. Christmas was coming to Ballynatroy. Once again the big market had fulfilled its promise.

MUSHA

———

THE LURCHER DROPPED THE STILL-QUIVERING BODY OF A HARE AT HIS MASTER'S FEET JUST MOMENTS BEFORE LORD HAILEY'S GAME KEEPER TOPPED THE RISE AT THE END OF THE WOOD'S FRINGE.

Mick Foley had barely commended the dog and picked up the dead animal when he saw him. "Cover," he hissed quickly to the well-trained hound, who vanished like a shadow into the trees, followed immediately by himself.

This was an oft-repeated manoeuvre and it was, in fact, flirting with death, as poachers were accorded no mercy on the Hailey estate. Personally, though, he preferred to risk his life in this exciting and rewarding way than to die a lingering death by the side of the road breaking stones for a wage that was barely enough to keep body and soul together. As it was, he ate like the Lord himself in Burnside Hall.

However, as he slipped silently through the wood, he nursed a growing suspicion that the game keeper was out to get him. He just seemed to be more active of late, especially in the approaches to the glen which sheltered his cabin. Perhaps he should lie low for a while…

When deep among the trees he paused and emitted a sharp, high whistle. After a couple of moments the lurcher emerged from the base of a mound of moss-grown rocks and dead leaves, which was the concealed entrance to an ancient souterain, and jumped up on him in a familiar ritual of greeting. "Good Boy, Musha," said his master, caressing him. I'm thinking maybe we'll rest you a while."

But there were a few good meals to come, none the less. He took the hare from under his coat and allowed Musha to sniff it. "You'll get your share, don't worry," he reassured the eager dog and they made tracks for home.

It was around noon the next day when calling voices disturbed the quiet of the glen. The sound of them brought Mick out of his cabin to investigate. He observed a line of people spaced at intervals covering the ground and calling "Jonathan, Jonathan," as they proceeded. On a closer approach Mick recognized servants and out-workers from the Hall and when one, a gardener whom he knew, drew near, he asked him what was afoot.

"The young master is lost," the man told him. "Tis feared he may be kidnapped, but no-one knows his fate." On being pressed for details he related how the nursemaid had been walking in the garden with the five-year-old boy and pushing his baby sister in her pram. Suddenly the baby had started to choke and have a fit, so the alarmed girl had picked her up and run into the house for help, telling young Jonathan to stay where he was. When the fuss had died down and the baby recovered, the boy could not be found. Everybody available had been summoned and they had been searching ever since.

"Well, he didn't come this way," said Mick, "or my dog would have heard him, surely."

But the searchers continued to comb the glen to no avail and late into the evening their calls could still be heard coming from the surrounding countryside.

It was, indeed, a mystery. But another mystery was occupying Mick's mind as the night drew in. Musha, in his turn, was missing. The dog was always in his place by the hearth at bedtime and his absence filled Mick with foreboding. Had he been shot? What else but injury, or death, would keep him from home?

After an uneasy night Mick set off at dawn on his own one-man search for the precious lurcher. As he went he gave the penetrating whistle that the animal always obeyed. But no Musha came bounding…

Then he was in the wood and heading for the souterain. If the dog was wounded, he thought, he might have crawled in there to die. Reaching the mound of stone, he whistled again. Then waited, holding his breath, listening for a sound. Sure enough, he was rewarded by a yelp. Overjoyed, he began to push aside the ferns and branches covering the entrance to the passage, at the same time calling to Musha to come out. But he could detect no movement from inside and when he paused to listen, he could just hear a faint whimpering.

Growing more and more anxious, now afraid that the dog was seriously hurt, he started to crawl into the tunnel. He knew from a previous investigation that it ended in a small chamber, from which further egress was blocked by fallen debris. He crawled on and finally felt open space in front of him. The whimpering increased and he stretched out a hand to feel around.

His hand encountered warm flesh! And it was not the dog's. He explored further - it was a human leg! At that point he felt the frantic licking of the dog's tongue on his hand and a child started to cry. Completely bewildered, Mick crawled further into the chamber until both hands were free to explore what confronted him. As far as he could make out in the pitch dark, Musha was curled around a small child, who was clutching tightly onto him. He made soothing noises and tried to prize the child away from the dog, but his efforts only resulted in louder wails.

What to do?

He concluded that he would have to try and drag the two inseparable bodies out of the souterain together. Accordingly, he got both arms around the bundle and reversed back into the passage. By dint of much dragging, soothing, licking and wailing, the extraordinary group finally emerged into the daylight.

Mick's astonished gaze took in the figure of a small boy, clothes crumpled and dirty, face and hair smeared with mud, who continued to wail and bury his face in the dog's neck.

Could this possibly be the missing Hailey heir? "Jonathan," he murmured into the boy's ear "Jonathan." The child stopped crying briefly and looked up at the man, who must seem like his captor. But his response confirmed Mick's notion that he must, indeed, be Jonathan Hailey. "Let's go home," he cajoled. "I'll carry you." He sat on the ground next to the two entwined bodies and very gradually, talking reassuringly all the time, he managed to transfer the little boy's grip to his own thick, dark hair and eased him up onto his shoulders. Then, with Musha in close attendance and constantly jumping up to bestow a lick onto a bare leg, they set off for the big house.

After some 25 minutes of proceeding in this manner, they reached the gates of Burnside Hall, which, unusually, stood open.

Thus, without hindrance, they entered and went up along the curving drive until the house came into view. Outside was a scene of commotion. Mick could see what looked like a platoon of soldiers, with mounted officers; there were policemen there and Lord Hailey himself, mounted on his big bay hunter.

Into this throng entered the strange little group. As soon as they were observed, a startled silence fell on the assembled people. Then there were gasps of amazement and a general surge forward towards the three. But Lord Hailey was the first to reach them, sliding down from his horse and approaching with rapid strides. Stopping in from of Mick, he held out his arms. "Jonathan, my son," he cried.

"Pa pa". The little boy allowed himself to be detached from the rescuer's shoulders, but he was no sooner in his father's arms, than he was reaching down to Musha and crying, "Wolf, wolf."

"What is the meaning of this"? Lord Hailey now addressed Mick, while trying to restrain the boy in his efforts to reach down to the jumping dog.

"Your Honour," said Mick. It's how I found the child in a cave in yon wood. It seems my dog, Musha, had guarded him all night and it was mighty hard to separate the two of them."

"Musha"! Jonathan had picked up on the name of the dog and he began to struggle so hard that his father had to put him down, whereupon the two fell on each other and once more became entwined as one.

Lord Hailey clapped a hand on Mick's shoulder. "Your name, my man?," he said. "You will be rewarded for your service."

Mick gave his name and his Lordship, noting the vice-like grip of his son on the dog, said, "And your price for the dog - it seems that the boy has taken to him."

"The dog is not for sale, Your Honour," Mick replied. "No price in the world would buy him."

Hailey looked bemused at that. Then an officer rode up and said, "You'll have no need of the search party, now that your son has returned, Sir?"

"No. Please dimiss everyone - and my sincere thanks to them all."

Meanwhile Jonathan had got to his feet and was trying to tug Musha in the direction of the house. But the dog was resisting and looking up to his master. It seemed like an impasse. The house servants had come out to rejoice in the safe return of the young heir, who had by then started to cry with frustration when the dog wouldn't budge and was ignoring everyone.

"What's to do, Foley?" His Lordship looked equally frustrated.

"I'll have to accompany the young lad, your Honour, and then the dog will come, too." Mick was no slouch when opportunity offered.

"Yes. That's it, I suppose." Hailey somewhat reluctantly moved aside and immediately Mick, child and dog moved forward.

Up the steps and in the front door of the mansion they went, bewildered servants and his Lordship following. In the great hall, at the foot of the marble staircase, stood Lady Hailey who, at the sight of her son, gave a cry and ran to take him in her arms. Jonathan suffered her embrace and started to chatter about his adventure - how he had got lost in the forest and had found a cave and how the wolf called Musha had kept him warm. And then the man had come and brought him home. "Now Musha's mine," he finished and struggled out of his mother's arms back to the dog. "We're hungry," he announced and in moments he was running off through the hall, followed by Musha, who seemed to have relaxed, now that he had brought his two humans to safety.

Lady Hailey was weeping with relief and her husband put his arm around her. "Don't cry, my dear, he said. "All's well that ends well - and this is the man we have to thank." He indicated Mick, who was standing unobtrusively near by. "A man whom, it appears, has become a necessary part of the household." He beckoned to the butler, who had remained standing by the door. "See that Foley is fed," he ordered, "and prepare accommodation for him."

"Yes, my Lord." The man indicated that Mick should follow him and as he did, he reflected happily that it was surely with God's help that within a few hours his status had changed from legitimate prey to protected species.

IN REMEMBRANCE

––––––––

THE OLD WOMAN SAT ROCKING GENTLY BY THE WINDOW IN THE MOONLIGHT, THE BEADS AND THE GOLDEN CRUCIFIX THAT DANGLED FROM HER FINGERS SPARKLING AS THEY WERE CAUGHT IN THE FITFUL BEAMS. IT WAS ON JUST SUCH A NIGHT AS THIS, SHE MUSED, THAT THEY HAD COME INTO HER POSSESSION. SHE RECALLED HER FIRST SIGHT OF INNISMACHA AFTER SHE, AS THE ELDEST OF THE McGILL FAMILY - AND THE ONE TO ENSURE THAT THE HOLDING OF LAND REMAINED IN IT - HAD BEEN DESPATCHED TO THE ISLAND TO EASE THE LAST DAYS OF GRANDFATHER MORONEY.

It had not been a prospect that she relished and the boatman who had conveyed her had seemed to echo her sentiments as he helped her ashore. 'God be with you, alanna', he had said. 'Tis a fierce lonesome station for a young lassie.

'It won't be for long, Mairtin', she had replied in her innocence. 'Only for the while that Grandad needs me'.

The old man had pushed off, muttering to himself, as she had turned to climb the steep path up from the water, hoping her brave words proved to be true. She had certainly not wanted to be stuck out on the island indefinitely. Tradition was strong in the isolated west, though, and in the early part of the century you did what your parents told you, even if you were nineteen or twenty.

At the top of the cliff path the white-washed cottage had come into view. Her grandfather had been sitting in a chair in the doorway and she had waved cheerfully to him, eliciting a raised arm in response. When she had reached him, his greeting had not been effusive and she was, in fact, soon to discover that he was a bag of grumbles.

He had lost no time in acquainting her with his current tribulations and in venting his ire on the cause of them - the customs officer. 'I don't get a moment's peace', he had complained. 'Day and night he's patrolling the island, looking for smugglers. 'Am I suspected of smuggling?' he had demanded peevishly, 'and me hardly able to move with the age! I wish the lot of them perdition,' he had concluded, 'smugglers and Revenue men, both'! and he had banged his stick on the flagstones as though he had had some of the offenders at his mercy.

Somewhat startled at this tirade, she had tried to soothe him. 'Come on inside, Grandad, and I'll wet some tea'. She had helped him up, 'I'll try to keep them from bothering you', she had said, as he had limped into the cottage. The old man had snorted, obviously having no more faith in her ability to do so than she actually had herself.

She had thought that perhaps the activity he described would make her stay less tedious, but it was not long before she had found out that her grandfather had good cause for complaint.

After she had settled him by the fire, she had decided to investigate the lie of the land and had set out across the island, of which Tadhg Moroney was the last inhabitant. It had an ancient history dating back many centuries to when a community of monks had established an abbey there, and she had wanted to explore the old ruins.

On approaching them she had been hailed by an authoritative voice, 'Stop, if you please, and explain your presence'!

Looking up, she had seen a uniformed officer cresting the hill to her right. Immediately she had felt anger flushing her cheeks. She had pushed back the unruly chestnut curls that framed her face and glared at him. 'What's it to you'? she had snapped. 'I'm on my grandfather's land'.

The customs man had approached closer. 'Your grandfather's property is under the jurisdiction of the Crown - like the rest of the country', he had said, barely disguising the sneer in the words. 'And if he is found to be collaborating with smugglers, he'll find himself in prison. You, too', he had finished, before turning and striding away, leaving her stunned and breathless with fury.

Then she had realized why the old man was so upset. Good luck to the smugglers, she had thought. If she could help them, she would.

Her opportunity to do so had come a few days later, when she was poking about in the ruins. In the old days the monks often constructed a stone chamber as a sweat house. This one was situated outside the walls of the enclosure and was concealed by low-growing scrub. She only found it because she had slipped on an adjacent rock and grabbed at the bushes to save herself. It was then she had noticed the narrow aperture and had crawled through. Part of the structure had collapsed and enough of the failing evening light had filtered through cracks in the stones for her to make out another opening, partly blocked by fallen debris.

Gingerly she had struggled through the crumbling gap and just when she could see faint light ahead of her, the loose shingle had given way and she had slithered down a rough slope, landing with a jolt and a cry of fear.

Before she knew where she was, a hand had been clapped over her mouth and a voice was hissing her to silence. Struggling and kicking instinctively, she had soon become aware that her efforts were to no avail and had given up the fight.

She had lain back and looked up at her captor. She had seen a wild-looking face, topped by a woolen cap from which jet-black strands of hair escaped to frame it. Slowly she had been released, the man had continued to crouch beside her and had pressed his fingers to his lips. 'Silence, please', he muttered hoarsely. 'There is much danger'. 'Who are you'? she had gasped.

'You can call me Jean-Baptiste', was the reply in low, heavily-accented tones. 'Perhaps you guess my business'? He had gestured round what had taken shape as a rocky cavern open to the sea, against the sides of which packages and cases were piled in profusion.

Smuggling', she had whispered, an exultant thrill making her shiver. So much now for the hated customs man! 'Yes - you will help me?' the smuggler had asked. 'I must load a boat. but first..

He had grabbed a package and ripped it open, extracting a small bottle. He had pulled out the stopper and with unexpected gentleness had dabbed some of the contents onto her wrists. Then he had pressed the bottle into her hand. 'For an Irish lady', he had said, 'the perfume of France. And now to work . . .'

She had gasped as the exotic scent had wafted about her. 'For me? Really? To Keep'? She had clutched the bottle as the Frenchman laughed and started to gather up the contraband. Between them they had transported the lot and loaded it into a boat that was moored to a small jetty.

When it was all stowed Jean-Baptiste had sprung lightly back to where she stood. 'Meet me at the same place, one week's time,' he had said and suddenly, without warning, he was kissing her. Then he was back in the boat and away with a wave, leaving her trembling at the edge of the water.

She couldn't remember how long she had stood there, staring at the vanishing wake of the boat. When all sight and sound of it had been swallowed up by the night, she had shaken her head and decided she must have been dreaming, until she brushed her hand across her eyes and smelt the proof of her adventure.

Then she had laughed wildly and bent down to scrub her wrists in the sea. If her grandfather's suspicions were aroused, she knew what the outcome would be - he might even talk to the customs in his desire to be rid of trouble.

As it was, he had looked at her strangely when she had returned. 'What kept you out this late'? he had grumbled. 'You don't want to be abroad after dark with queer comings and goings on the island'.

'I'm sorry Grandad. She had bustled about, hiding her nervous excitement by lighting the lamp and making tea. 'I was watching some seals'.

'Seals" he had muttered. 'Faith, it's more than seals that do be beyond in the bay'.

But the anxious moment had passed without more comments and later, in bed, she had dabbed some of the perfume on her pillow and relived the whole extraordinary scene.

Sitting in her chair by the dying embers of the fire, Maggie McGill could recall vividly the suppressed excitement she had felt during the intervening days - an excitement such as she had not experienced since. She smiled to herself as she thought how the experiences that were packed into that brief period had coloured the rest of her life - the experiences and the expectations, which had only lessened very, very gradually.

Even now, she half expected to hear a light footfall on the shingle path and a low, foreign voice exhorting her to silence. . .

The week of waiting had seemed more like a month, but at last the time had come. The old man had retired to bed when she had silently left the house. The smuggler was at work when she had reached the cavern, a sense of urgency in his movements. 'The Revenue cutter is out', he had said. 'We must work fast'.

She had quickly joined him and as they had prepared to carry out the last load, he had taken her in his arms and kissed her passionately. The he had fished in his pocket for a set of rosary beads, which he had pressed into her hand. 'Pray for me', he had said. 'And remember . . .' and before she had had time to speak, he was moving out urging, 'Hurry'.

He was already in the boat when the faint throb of an engine sounded in the distance. 'The cutter', she had gasped, as the Frenchman had pushed away from the jetty.

He had raised his hand in farewell. 'I'll be back', and he was gone into the gathering dark.

But he had said he'd be back, she had consoled herself. One day he would come again to the cavern. She would watch for him tomorrow, and all the tomorrows, until . . .

THE PILGRIMAGE

PETER BRADY PAUSED AS HE BREASTED THE FINAL EASY SLOPE
BEFORE TACKLING THE STEEP RISE TO THE SUMMIT OF THE
MOUNTAIN. HE LOOKED BACK AT THE STREAM OF PILGRIMS
TOILING UP THE STONY PATH BEHIND HIM AND ACROSS THE
BAY AS THE ISLANDS BEGAN TO EMERGE FROM THE DAWN MIST.
THE LAST TIME HE HAD CLIMBED CROAGH PATRICK IT HAD
BEEN AT NIGHT, BECAUSE THAT IS HOW THE PILGRIMAGE USED
TO BE UNTIL THE CHURCH HAD RULED OTHERWISE IN RECENT
TIMES. HE REMEMBERED THE TORCHLIGHT PROCESSION AND
THE SENSE OF GAIETY AND ADVENTURE, WHICH SOMEHOW
SEEMED TO BE LACKING IN THE DAYLIGHT CLIMB.

Or perhaps the missing ingredient was the girl. He
wondered if it was the lingering memory of that elfin face
that had inspired him to make the climb again after all those
years - years that had brought hard work, success and enough
money to retire on comfortably, but which somehow lacked
an anchor.

With a half sigh he turned again to face the steepest and
most dangerous part of the ascent, the part comprised of huge

loose boulders and small, sharp, slippery rocks, which caused many a fall and twisted ankle.

Because of the years spent on building sites, Peter found them easier to negotiate than he had expected from the last time but, as far as he could recall, coming down was more risky. It was on the descent that the girl in front of him had lost her footing and tumbled down the last few feet of the unstable peak. He had hastened after her and raised her up by the light of other pilgrims' torches and the rising moon. 'My ankle' she had said. 'It's broke, for sure'.

Half carrying her, he had got her to a steady rock out of the way of other climbers and sat her down while he felt for broken bones. Finally he had said, 'You've only wrenched it - a bit of a rest and you'll be back on your feet'.

'It's terrible sore', she had moaned. 'Don't leave me.'

And he hadn't left her then. Perhaps he never really had. As he clambered over the last few stones and reached the flat plateau on which the chapel stood, he thought that maybe it had been a mistake to return, that it would have been better to stay in England instead of coming back to claim the family home in Falduff, which he could see now, below in the distance.

Without a family, he was free to choose and doubt began to infiltrate his plans.

Back in another time, he allowed himself to be drawn to the chapel by the crowd now pressing around him, but he scarcely heard the words of the priest intoning Mass while he pondered on the future. Would he ever settle into village life again, or would he be better back in the city where he had come from and where his friends now were? It was in a state of confusion that Peter started back down the mountain. He thought he recognized the rock where he had sat with the girl so long ago. They had stayed there until the day had dawned and from time to time he had massaged her ankle, which had swelled up a little and shown some bruising.

As the light dawned, he could see that her hair was red beneath a woolen cap, that her heart-shaped face was covered in freckles and that her eyes were as green as the deepest sea pool.

Her name was Janey, she had told him, and she lived beyond in Castlebar, where her father had a pub. She had made the climb with some girl friends, but they had gone on ahead and goodness knew how she would find them now, or get back home.

He'd see her right, he had said. And he had told her about himself. Of the family home at Falduff, of his three sisters and his brother and of the sheep they ran on the hill. There was not a living in it for all of them, he had explained, which was why he was headed for England the very next day. His brother could have the farm and, really, he was welcome to it.

Would he not miss home? she had asked. Would he not miss climbing the mountain and seeing the islands below like jewels in the bay? Would he not miss the soft voices of Mayo and the mists that caressed the meadows? She had heard, she said, that England was a hard land that could break your heart.

He certainly had missed all these intangible things, Peter reflected. All those things that together made the sum total of Mayo. Wasn't that why he was back here now? All the same, the hard country had paid off and he had lived there well enough for nigh on forty years.

But at the time he had shrugged off the questions. 'What's the alternative?' he had answered. 'We cannot all live off the land'.

As the light had grown they had started on the journey down the mountain. The girl was able to put a little weight on her foot and with his arm about her and the aid of a stick they had made slow progress downwards.

Strands of her hair had brushed his face and every now and then a gasp of pain had caused him to tighten his arm, pressing her body against his own. By the time they reached the first station, his senses were drunk with her nearness and he wanted to hold her forever.

But a bus was waiting at the inn at the end of the trail and he had to hand her up into it and see her settled in a seat. 'Thank you, Peter Brady', she had said. 'I'll not forget your kindness. And if you miss that boat to England, I'll be here'.

He had not missed the boat to England, but for a long time afterwards his dreams had been haunted by that elfin face looking from the window of the bus as it drove away, taking her out of his life.

As he proceeded down the mountain, he became more and more sure that it had been a mistake to come back. With property at a premium, he would have no trouble selling the farm, even though it had been untended since his brother's death the previous year.

With the money he could buy an apartment and never hear again the soft, insinuating voices of Mayo, particularly the one that had spoken of the islands like jewels and the misty meadows.

Reaching the inn at the bottom, he called for a drink to be brought outside and sat at a table, watching the throng of pilgrims coming and going.

His drink arrived and someone sat down opposite him. Glancing round, he saw that it was the woman from the bar and he groped in his pocket for the money. The she spoke. 'So you caught the boat to England, Peter Brady'.

Startled, he looked at her again - and he saw, beneath the lines of care, a freckled, heart-shaped face, out of which shone two green green eyes beneath hair, now cropped and faded, but with still a hint of once-vivid red. 'Janey', he breathed. 'You remembered me! But how did you know …?

She laughed: 'You forget what it's like to live in a small community. The moment you drove up in your fine Mercedes, the word was out that the big contractor was home to stay'.

'They know more than I do, then'. He was nonplussed and his heart was racing in a way that the climb did not account for. 'And what of you'? he asked. 'Has life been good to you'?

She looked away and he could see the knuckles of her hands turn white as she clasped them together. 'Well, yes and no to that', she replied. 'I married, but my husband died and my two children are grown and I work here now when they need a hand. I had the experience, you know'.

He remembered that her people had kept a pub in Castlebar. 'I got the place in Falduff', he told her. 'But I don't know yet will I stay'.

'Your family … are they abroad in England still?'

'I'm on my own', he said. 'I have no family'.

He watched her hands relax and then she laughed and got up. 'Well, mind you don't miss the boat this time, either, Peter Brady'.

'Janey'. He got to his feet. 'What time are you free?'

'Around six', she said.

'I'll be here'. If he hurried, there'd be time to get the place half decent, to prepare a meal, to get some flowers … He gunned the powerful car and as he drove he thought of the mist on the meadows, and the sea, and all the things that made Falduff the most beautiful place on earth and the final haven for two lonely pilgrim.

A STATUE FOR COMPANY

───────

I T WAS ANOTHER DAY IN THE GLEN, BUT FOR MARY ELLEN LYNCH THERE WAS NO REASON TO SUPPOSE THAT IT WOULD BE ANY DIFFERENT FROM THE TWO THOUSAND DAYS THAT HAD PRECEDED IT SINCE THE DEATH OF HER MOTHER.

She let the hens out of the barn and called to the dog to fetch the cow for milking. The sun slowly penetrated the mist and illuminated the valley, eventually hinting at the lakes which nestled far below in the bogs that lay between the Glen and Clifden. To the eye of a stranger it would have been a magical scene, but familiarity breeds contempt and Mary Ellen had been familiar with it for all of her thirty years.

The social system in rural Ireland decreed that the head of the household could name whichever of his offspring he chose to inherit the family-holding, and the custom was for the favourite son to have it signed over to him on his marriage - to a bride of the father's choosing. But the tendency was for him to delay this legality - sometimes for too long, so that death intervened to prevent anyone from becoming the new owner.

This had happened in the Lynch's case and Mary Ellen's five siblings had left home in disgust to seek a living elsewhere, consoled by the presumption that their younger sister would be content to remain in the Glen and look after their mother.

And the reason for their assumption became apparent as she positioned the milking stool beneath Maggie, the cow, and bent her head into the animal's side: the oblique rays of the sun fell directly onto the right side of her face, causing the strawberry mark, which stretched from the hairline to below the chin, to glow with an almost fluorescent brilliance. This, then, was what had kept the young woman in the remote homestead and made of her a virtual hermit.

The only time she emerged from her mountain fastness was to attend Mass on Sunday, when she would descend the long twisting road on her rickety bicycle to the village on the main road where, with a scarf covering most of her face, she could enter the church without speaking to anyone.

She would leave in the same way and, never having heard her speak, the villagers regarded her as Mad Mary Ellen.

But the elderly parish priest knew very well that she was not crazy, although the question as to how long she would retain her sanity in her self-imposed isolation was one that bothered him exceedingly.

The particular morning referred to continued to unfold as Mary Ellen went about her chores. To a large extent she was self-supporting: her potato patch, recently sprayed, showed healthy-looking blossoms and lay, along with the vegetables, within the confines of a circular way; the hens provided eggs, the cow milk and butter.

Mad Mary Ellen's was not a place where anyone would be encouraged to linger.

She straightened up from weeding the carrots and as she did so her eye caught a movement far down on the rutted road. Shading her eyes with her hand, she could just make out a solitary figure with a dog in close attendance. She stared anxiously - what would bring a stranger up the long road into the Glen?

Eventually the walker appeared. He held the dog on a lead and carried a bag in his other hand.

Instinctively her hand went up to her blemished face. She turned and hurried back into the house, where she snatched her scarf off the back of the door and tied it tightly round her head. Then she watched as they reached the little gate that stood open at the end of her path and there they paused. The dog whined and the man set down his bag. He was youngish - about her own age, Mary Ellen reckoned. He had a felt hat pulled down over his eyes and from beneath which some locks of brown hair had escaped. Then he spoke "God save all here", he said. "May I step in for a while?" His accent was not a local one.

"You'll be looking for the Joyces", Mary Ellen said, stepping into the shade of the door.

"It's maybe yourself I'd sooner talk to", he replied, and without more ado picked up his bag and, with the dog in front, proceeded towards her.

Mary Ellen shrank backwards. She had simply never visualized a stranger crossing the threshold, but this one made towards the hearth and hooked his leg around a chair, dragging it into position, and then seated himself, his hand on the head of the dog, who sat by his side panting. "Could I trouble you for a dish of water for my friend here?" he said. "That hill would put a thirst on man and beast. It's a mighty lonesome place for a lovely young girl like yourself to be living", he remarked then.

Mary Ellen flushed. Was he making fun of her, or what? "Well, if it is, what'd bring the likes of you up into it?" she demanded somewhat tartly, clattering the delph unnecessarily.

"Sure, I thought you might like one of my holy figures for company". He released the catch of the bag and took out a selection of plaster saints, "They're not dear at all and wouldn't a couple of them look fine on the mantelpiece?"

Mary Ellen stopped in her tracks. There was no overmantle - just a wide open hearth. Did he, too, think she was crazy? She put the cup of tea on the table. "Let you take you tea and be on your way", she said. "What use would I have for ornaments?"

The would-be salesman let his hands fall. He re-wrapped the figures and put them back in the bag before turning round to face her again.

"That's a harsh thing to say". He spoke sadly. "Wouldn't one of them saints only reflect your own fair beauty?" He reached out for the cup, but misjudged the distance, knocked it over with the tea spreading in a brown stain over the oilcloth.

Mary Ellen jumped backwards to avoid being scalded. "Why don't you look what you're doing? Is it blind you are?" she exclaimed in vexation. She looked up to meet his unwavering gaze - eyes wide open, but not registering - and the truth hit her: the way he followed the dog, the way he had felt for the chair, the compliments he had paid to her beauty despite her disfigurement.

"I'm sorry". They said it together.

"I'm all thumbs", he said.

She poured a fresh cup, added milk and sugar and placed it touching his hand, holding it until his fingers closed around it. She buttered a slice of soda bread and put the plate on his knee. "Let you quench your thirst now", she urged him softly. "And here's a bite to go along with it".

"Thank you". As if he sensed her sudden sympathy, he lowered his head and plied himself to the bread and tea.

Shock waves went through Mary Ellen. At the same time she felt a strange elation. For the first time in her life she was meeting a stranger who regarded her as normal - a young man who actually thought she was lovely. Impulsively she wrenched at her scarf and threw it in a corner. She mopped up the table, then moved to face him across the hearth. "I might have one of them statues, after all", she decided out loud.

The young man smiled, transforming his face beneath the untidy brown hair. "You'll not regret it", he said. "Rich and poor alike do be buying them off me - the house that has one will surely be blessed". He finished the tea and felt for the table.

Mary Ellen took the cup out of his hand. "Do you travel far, then?" she asked.

"I come from Donegal", he said, "the home of the O'Donnells. A beautiful place - for those with eyes to see".

Mary Ellen felt confused, now that his affliction was directly referred to. She remained silent.

"And what name is on yourself?" came the soft enquiry.

"Mary Ellen Lynch". She found her tongue.

"Folk call me Cel", he told her then. "'Tis short for Celestine, which is an awkward sort of a name".

"I like that", she said. "It has a lovely sound to it".

The dog at his feet stirred. "I'm thinking poor Jack is hungry", said his master, releasing the lead. "Would there be a few scraps he could have?"

Jack rubbed against her, looking up eagerly and ignoring a suspicious growl from her own collie. She shooed her dog out and mashed up some left-over potatoes with a dash of buttermilk. Jack took no time in devouring the meal and then started to investigate the premises.

Cel opened his bag again and felt among the statues. "Let you be choosing one now", he said.

Mary Ellen knelt down as he began to lift them out. "This is St. Brigid", he said, running his finger confidently over them as he undid the wrapping. "This is the Virgin herself ... this is St. Therese ...

Mary Ellen inspected them carefully. "I'll have St. Therese", she finally announced.

"You made the right choice", was the reply, "for isn't she just like you, who'll be owning her, young and fair and beautiful?"

His listener's heart contracted - what harm that she was neither so young, nor beautiful, and that her hair was actually black? At that moment she felt beatified, like the saint.

He held the statue towards her and as she clasped it their hands met. Mary Ellen did not draw back. Since her mother died, no other human being had touched her. She remained quite still as his hand traveled up her arm and reached her face; even as his fingers touched her livid cheek, she made no move, but held her breath as he caressed it.

"Oh, Mary Ellen" - a sigh came from deep down inside him. "You feel so good", he murmured. "Better than all the saints in Heaven".

Time stood still until an excited bark from outside broke the spell. Shame began to replace wonder as Mary Ellen got to her feet - it was surely a sin to let a man's hands on her. And to like it. She shook her head. "What brought you here, Celestine O'Donnell?" she asked in anguish. "What possessed you to follow the long road to the Glen?"

The blind pedlar gave a little laugh. "Why, it was Father O'Grady directed me", he replied. "He said there was a lovely young girl up here in sore need of a statue for company".

The two dogs burst into the room, panting, and settled down by the hearth, as though they knew it was the most natural thing in the world to be together.

FROM CARRIAGE TO
ASS AND CART

TIGHE McCURTAIN WHISTLED SOFTLY BETWEEN HIS TEETH AS HE MADE HIS WAY ALONG THE OVERGROWN AVENUE THAT LED UP TO THE DERELICT MANSION, IN THE PAST THE HOME OF THE ONCE PROUD ST. LAWRENCE FAMILY.

He was no stranger to the shaggy woodlands on either side, as they had yielded many a rabbit for his solitary pot and the drive itself he knew like the back of his hand from the countless times he had driven the coach along it. Now he was on his way to investigate a rumour that someone was living in the old house. It hardly seemed possible to his way of thinking, seeing how it was twenty years since Lord St. Lawrence had died and his only remaining relative, his daughter Harriet, had gone off to foreign parts. Much of the roof had capsized in the meantime and the wind sighed unchecked through the broken windows and along the corridors once filled with bustling staff.

Many of them were dead now, too, along with his own wife, who had been the personal maid of Miss Harriet - a position which no one had envied her, Harriet being an arrogant miss. No loss, indeed, had been in evidence when the said Harriet, sole heir to her father's estate, had chosen to depart the district, thus sounding the death knell of the big house.

Tighe had often regretted it, though. He had loved to drive the pair of spanking bays, bringing her ladyship, before her last illness, to visit the other great houses of the area; he had enjoyed the gossip in the kitchens and the sparkle of great social occasions. It was a lonely old life now, although there was something to be said for being one's own boss - not having to take orders and bow and scrape to the nobility . . . so his thoughts ran, as he scuffed through the leaves and tried to avoid the ruts on the driveway.

Past another bend and the house came into sight, staring with blind eyes at the encroaching wilderness. He crossed the sweep of weed-engulfed gravel and slowly climbed the mossy front steps. The glass panels by the side of the door were broken and he peered through, but could see nothing in the gloomy interior. Then, as he turned to go away, he fancied he heard a low moan. "Is anyone within"? he called, and waited. There was no answer except, perhaps, another faint moan. He decided to go round to the back and find an entrance in the region familiar to him of old. All was as dark and derelict as he expected, but the back door gave to his push and he stepped inside to the stone-flagged passage.

Calling again and feeling his way in the gloom, he bypassed the servants' quarters to reach the back stairs. Again, a distinct sound of distress came to him and he moved faster.

There at the foot of the stairs was a dark awkward bundle, covered in plaster and splinters. His hands pushed through the debris of the collapsed stairway and elicited a sharp cry, "My legs!" Scraping off the rubble quickly, he found the main pillar of the banister lying across the lower part of the woman's body, trapping her legs. "God's tooth!" he exclaimed. "Let ye be still while I lift this off".

Bracing himself against the wall, he heaved at the timber until it shifted and the woman's legs were freed. A portion of the steps had partly supported it, keeping the brunt of its weight off the inert form. He now rolled her clear. "Can ye sit up, at all?" he asked, getting his arm under her shoulders.

He could see the woman was about his own age. She looked frail in the dim light and was bundled up in dark clothes. She made an effort to sit up and her hands went to her legs. "Not broken at least", she muttered.

"Help me . . . "

Tighe put an arm round her waist. "Let you lean on my shoulder", he said and in that way they shuffled along the passage until they reached the servants' hall, which, he noticed, showed signs of recent habitation and a fire had been lit. He lowered his burden onto a rickety chair and stepped back.

"Is it staying here you are, Ma'am"? he finally asked.

The figure in the chair stayed slumped over. Dishevelled hair framed a haggard face that was streaked with dust and grime from her fall. But she looked up at his question. "You are Tighe McCurtain", she said, and her voice had an echo of authority.

Tighe was mystified. How did this forlorn stranger know his name? He knew no one like her. He asked, "And what might your own name be, Ma'am"? a weak sigh was his answer, and Tighe thought he saw tears gathering at the corners of lowered eyes. In a broken voce she said, "You knew me as Harriet St. Lawrence a long time ago".

Tighe was stunned. He felt moidhered, as he might have expressed it himself. How could this miserable, sick-looking, lost soul be the daughter of his master, Lord Bartley St. Lawrence? As if she felt an explanation was due, the low voice continued, "My father left only debts - now my friends are all gone . . ." and suddenly the tears overflowed and sobs shook the frail body as shock set it.

Overcome by a wave of sympathy, Tighe knelt beside her, cradling her head. "Let you not take on, Ma'am," he soothed. "I'll look after you. You can come home with me." After a while the sobs abated and Tighe stood up. He bent and raised the former society belle to her feet and dusted off her clothes. "Have you any belongings"? he asked.

"There's a coat and there's a case in the corner." Tighe collected them, his throat constricting as he saw the initials on the worn leather case. H. St. L.

"Can you walk now"? he asked, steadying her with one arm.

"I'll manage", was the uncertain reply. But when she tried to stand, she winced with pain and sank back down into the chair.

Tighe was troubled. How was he going to convey her to his cottage - it was much too far to carry her. There was only one thing for it, he would have to fetch his ass and cart. "You just wait here, Ma'am", he told Harriet, "while I fetch a conveyance". She accepted his decision meekly and drew the coat he had passed her round her shoulders, resigned to whatever else fate had in store.

It was an hour and a half, or thereabouts, before her 'coachman' arrived back with his steed. With little preamble, he loaded her case into the cart and lifted herself in after it, arranging her on a pile of sacks. Then he led the animal off, jolting down the rutted drive - an ignominious journey compared with former ones behind the lively bays.

Back at his humble cottage on the side of Mt. Darragh, Tighe lifted his passenger down and supported her inside. He sat her down by the fire and brewed tea, lacing it generously with poitin. Harriet remained silent and when she had finished, Tighe commanded her to roll down her stockings, while he rubbed her injured legs with more of the spirits. She obeyed his commands docilely and in a short while regained her strength.

He gave her the double bed in the tiny room where he and his wife had slept and himself moved to the coilleach. As the days went by, the two conversed little, but Harriet learned to perform the daily tasks and to keep the cottage clean. After a day's work in the bog, or on the holding, she would have the potatoes boiled and maybe a poached fish, or a rabbit, along with them when he got home. He became used to her company and glad to have someone to share the loneliness of the glen.

The parish priest approached him one holy day after Mass and said, "I hear you've taken a woman into your house, Tighe. That is a grave sin in the eyes of Almighty God. You must either marry her or get rid of her." Tighe was stunned. Either course of action was unthinkable. He went home in a daze.

But it seemed as if the solution had been taken out of his hands. He was hardly in the door when he was met by Harriet. She looked very sprightly, he thought. The wholesome food and the mountain air had certainly put life back into her, but his problem only grew more acute. She was holding a letter in her hand. "A cousin has written to me, Tighe", she was saying. "Someone I had forgotten about in the north of the country. She invites me to make my home with her." Tighe felt a terrible tightening in his heart. He took a step forward. "No, Harriet", he said, calling her by name for the first time. "No. You cannot do that. Marry me instead!"

The letter, written by herself, fluttered to the floor as Tighe took her hand in his rough one - it didn't occur to him at all that no letters were ever delivered on a holy day.

THE ORPHANS

'SACRED HEART!' THE EXCLAMATION, FOLLOWED BY A THUMP, AS THE BAG OF TURF SLID OFF THE WOMAN'S BACK AND HIT THE GROUND, STARTLED THE COCK AND THE HENS THAT WERE SCRATCHING ROUND THE COTTAGE DOOR SO THAT THEY SET UP A CACKLING.

The author of the curse hopped about, muttering. Then she sat on the spilled bag and pulled off her boot to rub the stubbed toe. After a while she got up, still grumbling to herself, gathered up the turf and lugged the heavy load inside.

She built up the fire, then sat by the hearth to draw her breath. The place was getting too much for her, she realised, now that the pleasure of being her own mistress since the passing of the old folk had worn off. She was not getting any younger, either. During the time she had spent working on the farm, she reflected, the years had passed her by; she would never now have a family of her own - the voices of children would not in the future echo round the McLaren farm.

She wondered should she get rid of the three bullocks at the Michaelmas fair. With neither kith nor kin to share the burden of the place, she would be hard put to tend the lot. A too-adventurous hen crossed the threshold and she got up to shoo it out. The sun was at its zenith, lighting up the wide valley below the cottage and giving the golden thatch and the white-washed walls an almost metallic sheen. But the woman was unaware of the beauty inherent in the scene, nor of her own contribution to it, as she stood in the doorway, flapping her apron at the hens. She stood tall, with muscles that were honed from hard work, and her face was strong and topped by a crop of hair that still clearly showed its original raven colour. Her vivid blue eyes, now screwed up against the sunlight, surveyed the landscape - and came abruptly to rest on a figure that was toiling slowly up the stony boreen.

She watched, bemused, as the person, whom she could now see to be an unknown man, came ever nearer. He could be going nowhere but to the farm, as the boreen ended at the cottage. She remained at the door until finally, out of breath, the stranger stopped at the gate. He was carrying a small bag. 'I'm looking for a Mrs. McLaren', he said in an American accent.

The woman assessed him. A well set up man in a tweed suit, probably in his fifties, with grey hair beneath a peaked cap and a pleasant, if purposeful expression. 'This is the McLaren farm, all right', she replied eventually. 'But Mrs. McLaren is dead these twelve months. I'm Mary Jo' she added, 'and if I can help you, I will'.

'That's mighty kind of you', said the man. 'But I guess I'm a year too late'. It was his turn to regard her appraisingly. 'All the same', he concluded, 'we might very well have something to discuss'.

'Let you come in, then, and welcome'. Her curiosity aroused and still bewildered by the unexpected visitor. Mary Jo stood aside to let him in the door.

He stepped in and stood, cap in hand, looking around. 'It's a real nice place you've got here', he said. And then he smiled. It transformed his face, taking years away from it and expressing a boyish eagerness. impossible to resist.

Mary Jo smiled back. 'It's small', she replied. 'But it's plenty big for one'.

'You're by yourself?' the visitor asked in reply. 'May I sit down?'

'Of course - yes'.

He took one of the chairs by the hearth and she sat opposite him. After a brief silence, he spoke. 'I am called Tom Bryson', he said. 'I am an American citizen. My home was a good one and I lacked for nothing, but I always felt that something was missing. No matter what I achieved, I was still searching for something. I never married, because that did not seem the answer'.

He paused and Mary Jo leaned forward. 'Did you ever find it?' She was already caught up in the story.

'Yes, i did'. The american shifted his gaze from the burning turf and looked into her eyes. 'Three years ago i found what it was that seemed to haunt me. Just before my mother died, she told me that I was adopted, that I had an Irish mother and that the Nuns had sold me to them when I was a small baby'.

'Oh no'? Mary was appalled. Sure, Nuns would never be so heartless. But Tom Bryson certainly seemed to believe it. 'What then'? she encouraged him to continue.

'It's taken me all that time', he said, 'to trace my natural mother. 'She was Bridget Spillane from Drummin in Co. Mayo, and she ended up marrying Patrick McLaren - from this very farm, I do believe'.

Mary Jo sat in stunned silence, trying to absorb the implications of what he had told her. Had he come to claim the place? was he a McLaren? Had his mother married his father? Where did that leave her?

As if reading her thoughts, the American said, 'So that makes us brother and sister - or, at any rate, half ones, as we cannot know that we have the same father'.

'I suppose so'. Mary Jo was extremely doubtful how to react. She didn't know whether to be pleased, or frightened. To cover her confusion, she jumped up. 'You'll likely want to have a look round?' she offered and when he nodded, she led him outside and on by the meadow and across to the wetlands. She pointed out the grazing fields, the stony hillside that was fit only for sheep, and they looked into the brook, where trout could be caught and where there was said to be gold, washed down from the Sheffrey Mountains, 'I never found any, though', she confessed.

Bryson stopped. The shadows were lengthening now and a faint mist gave the mountains an ethereal look - a faeryland quality that perhaps their name Sheffrey, celebrated. 'Mary Jo', he said seriously, 'you don't have to look very far, it's all around you. This place is beautiful beyond anything I ever imagined. It's what was missing all my life, hidden in some secret corner of me, waiting patiently to be discovered'.

It was all too familiar to his companion, but she was pleased, none the less, that this visitor from far away should find it good. In fact, she liked him well enough; she liked his boyish smile, his direct manner and his eagerness - but the startling possibility of his relationship still scared her too much to let her relax. All the same, he would not find her lacking in hospitality. 'We'll be getting the tea now, when we go back', she said. 'I hope it will be to your liking, as well'.

'I guess it will be fine', was the reply, 'if it's not too much trouble'.

'You're welcome', she told him and back home did her best to overcome her misgivings - setting the table, collecting fresh eggs from the barn, slicing the soda bread, laying out the golden butter . . . It was enjoyable, she thought, or would be under different circumstances, entertaining a guest - entertaining a man! This new thought made her blush, for she had never previously had such an experience.

After the meal, which her guest declared he had enjoyed like none other, and she had seen to her chores, they pulled their chairs up to the bright hearth and Tom Bryson told her of his life with a New England couple, lacking for nothing and yet with the strange hunger at the back of it.

It became late with the telling and Mary Jo wondered what her guest had in mind. Finally she said, 'You'll be wanting a bed for the night?'

He hesitated before replying. Then, 'I'd be mightily obliged', he said. 'And seeing as we are brother and sister, there'd be no scandal in it'.

Things were moving very fast, thought Mary Joe. She felt drawn towards the stranger, but anxiety still predominated. What were his plans? He seemed kindly - surely she would not be evicted? Thinking these thoughts, she prepared the only bedroom. She herself slept in the colleach, or bed in the curtained niche by the fire. She lit a lamp and wished him goodnight, but it was a long time before she closed her own eyes.

In the morning she was astir early. She had the fire glowing and thick slices of bacon were sizzling on the pan, while the kettle steamed on the hob when the American opened his door. He was in his shirt-sleeves and unshaven and looked more at home in the surroundings. He was settling in quickly, she thought, with a pang of unease. Her own face was flushed from her efforts with the fire and tendrils of curling hair had escaped from their bonds to frame it.

She couldn't know it, but the picture she formed was older than history and as beautiful as femininity itself. It took Bryson's breath away and he stood in the doorway so long that she finally said tartly, 'Sit down, if you've a mind to, and be taking a bite'.

'This is lovely', he said, drawing up a chair, 'You know, it's a scene I'll carry in my mind all the way back to New York and afterwards'.

So he was going back. Now that he had stated his intention, Mary Jo found herself wishing he would stay. Her life had been so empty before he suddenly came into it. And it would be again when he left. 'You're pleased you came, then?' Some reply seemed called for.

His boyish smile was her answer. But then he spoke. 'Pleased, yes. Kind of sad, too . . . ' He broke off. '

'Sad?' She looked at him questioningly.

He started again. 'It's that I'm beginning to wish we weren't brother and sister, at all. If things were different, I believe we could be something more'.

The flush on Mary Jo's face deepened. She looked at her plate. Then she looked back up at him. 'I didn't like to tell you', she said. 'I thought you might be disappointed. I'm not your sister, at all. I'm no McLaren just an orphan, whom they fostered. Your mother had no other children'.

Bryson laid down his knife and stretched out his hand to her. 'That makes two, of us, then', he said.

'Yes'. Happiness spread over Mary Jo's face. She did not withdraw her hand, as she let the thought fill her mind of two halves that might finally become a whole.

THE RELIC

———

HOW CAN WE RISK OUT LAST FEW SHILLINGS ON A HORSE" MOANED KATE DEVANEY, "WHEN IT'S ALL WE HAVE BETWEEN US AND HARM."

"It's harm will befall us, anyway," retorted her husband, Ted, "with no money for the rent to be got, high or low. We'll be out on the road come Michaelmas, if we can't pay up."

Their 16-year-old daughter, Meg, added her voice to the dispute. "They do say the Squire's horse is unbeatable." she said. "We have little to lose, in any case, I could be away now to the race course and lay on the money." she concluded hopefully.

Ted looked at his wife, who gave him a long moment. Then, muttering to herself, the woman got on a chair, reached up to the top of the dresser and produced an object wrapped in a strip of red flannel. This she handed carefully to Meg. "Let you take this relic of St. Féchín and rub it on the legs of the horse," she said. "If the blessed saint doesn't help us this day, no other will."

Meg accepted the relic tentatively. "What is it, at all?" she asked uneasily.

"Tis a rib of St. Féchín," said her mother, Kate. "The only thing now that'll keep us off the road."

The girl tucked the relic down the front of her dress without more ado. Her father gave her a handful of shillings tied up in a rag and she was off running, her bare legs flashing as she skipped from tussock to tussock across the hillside, black curls blowing in the breeze.

"God go with her." The old woman back in the cabin crossed herself.

"And with the Squire's mare," replied her husband.

The race course was situated some two miles away on the 'flats,' an area of flat land by a river. When Meg arrived, the meeting was in full swing. People were milling about everywhere round the white-painted rails that encircled the course.

She found her way to a booth where bets were being taken and handed over her twist of shillings for a win for Autumn Plum, which was Squire Hendry's horse. If it did, indeed win, she would be the richer for £10 - a large sum in those days and one that would see her family secure for the year ahead.

Autumn Plum's race was the next but one, which left her time to locate the mare and give it the magic rub. She set off through the crowd to begin her search. She knew what the horse looked like, having seen it carrying the Squire round his demesne many times. She also knew that his racing colours were green and purple, so the search was not too daunting.

Horses were being led and ridden around by their jockeys and she climbed onto the back of an empty cart by one of the booths to get a better view. She scanned the scene. And then she spotted the colours she was looking for. The jockey was down beside the rails, watching the runners for the next race preparing.

He was talking to another rider, who stood next to him, and both of them were holding the reins of their mounts, which stood lined up behind them. Now was her chance.

She clamoured down and slipped through the crowd, landing up just at the back of the two horses, the one chestnut, the other black.

Stealing between them, she felt for the relic and withdrew it from its safe-keeping. She unwrapped the small, curved bone reverently and with her right hand began to pass it down the chestnut's flank. The horse stood quietly until she came to a point just above its fetlock, when it suddenly raised its hoof and flicked the bone out of her hand towards its black neighbour, hitting it on the hock.

That horse jerked up its foot and horror of horrors, put it down onto the priceless relic, leaving only the end of the bone protruding.

Overcome with dismay, Meg knelt on the ground and tried to tug the relic out. The horse refused to move its foot and as she continued her frantic efforts to retrieve it, she heard the black horse's jockey speaking.

"Let you pull your mare back," he was saying. "The odds on mine are much greater and, along with the bonus I'll collect from my master, we can share our winnings and be better off."

"I don't know." The other rider didn't sound too keen. "'Tis well known that mine's the better horse and if she doesn't win, it's meself that'll get lambasted."

"Oh, come on," urged the first voice. "The horse has run too many races - she's wore out. Just make it seem she's tired, like."

After a long pause, during which Meg was frozen to the ground, Autumn Plum's rider agreed. "All right, so. And it's the winnings halved."

"Done," said the other and at that moment the horses in the race that had been pending thundered by, capturing their attention and disturbing the black one that was crushing the relic. At last it shifted its foot and with one final tug, Meg retrieved the splinter that had survived the crush, picked herself up and was jostled away in the direction of the winning post by the crowds cheering the winner of the race.

She felt complete despair. She edged her way out of the mainstream and sat down on an upturned barrel beside a tent. As she re-wrapped the remains of St. Féchín in the red flannel, tears started from her eyes. How was she ever going to face home, with the money gone and the relic destroyed? May St. Féchín strike the evil jockey who was going to pull his horse! she mouthed silently.

For what seemed like an age she remained on her seat, sunk in misery. Then a yell of "They're off"! roused her and she realised that it must be the start of the race that was to have changed the family fortune - Autumn Plum's certain victory...

Almost against her will, she was drawn to the railings. The horses had to make two circuits of the track and there were six runners in the race.

It was easy for Meg to pick out the Squire's big chestnut and the unknown black horse and by the time the first circuit was completed, those two were leading the field, almost neck and neck.

Meg waited for the inevitable to happen - for Autumn Plum to fall back and allow the black to take the race. Sure enough, as she strained to see the furthest reaches of the course, she could make out the black pulling away in front and she silently prayed to St. Féchín for a miracle. But the saint seemed oblivious to her desperation and the black increased its lead. As they approached her on the final lap, a good length separated the two horses, when suddenly the black faltered and in a couple of lengths it had come to a standstill.

The other horses galloped by, but now the chestnut had a clear lead and seemed certain to win. Meg could hear the black's jockey cursing his mount and applying the whip - to no avail.

The horse was standing on three legs and refused to budge an inch. Finally the jockey dismounted and examined the foot that seemed to be injured. He poked about in the hoof and appeared to extract some object, after which it seemed no longer tender and the rider was able to lead it away. The foot was, Meg noticed, the one that had so mercilessly ground the relic to bits.

But at the moment all that concerned her was to collect the money. At last she had it in her hand - the ten pounds that would save the family from disaster. It truly did seem a miracle.

And as she stood there marveling, she became aware of the talk around her. "Twas a weakness in Black Prince's leg that caused it," "I heard it was how he twisted the fetlock," "sure, he mightened have won, anyway," "Wasn't he way in front, man! They say 'Twas a splinter in the foot that pulled him up."

Then Meg knew that it had indeed been a miracle that had saved the race for Autumn Plum. St. Féchín himself had surely driven the piece of his relic into the foot of the black horse to prevent his rider from achieving a false win!

With a joyous heart and a wondrous tale to tell, she made short shrift of the journey home.

THE SETTLEMENT

————

"OUCH"! WITH A WINCE OF PAIN, THE YOUNG WOMAN STRAIGHTENED UP FROM TENDING THE GRAVE. HER APPEARANCE BELIED HER YEARS, FOR SHE LOOKED TOIL-WORN AND DISHEVELED AND HER FACE HAD A DESOLATE EXPRESSION IN KEEPING WITH HER SURROUNDINGS.

The small enclosure containing a half dozen graves surmounted with simple wooden crosses was dominated by the square stone building of the church, the door of which had fallen away from its hinges and partly blocked the entrance. A few of the stones had become dislodged from the gable and swallows had flown in to nest in the rafters. It was three years since Parson Jones had preached his last sermon in it.

Maisie O'Hara did not linger in the graveyard, though, after she had attended to the double plot occupied by her foster parents. She hurried back along the rutted dirt road past the tiny empty cottages, which the vigorous undergrowth was already reclaiming.

The end one was where she lived. It was tidy enough, with a little gate opening onto a gravel path leading to the door and a clean-swept door step. Inside, the flagstones were scrubbed and a patchwork quilt on the 'coilleach' was a bright splash in the little room. The old couple had occupied the bedroom beyond until death had carried off, first Will McBride at the age of 78 and, one year later, Nonie, who had been 75. "God help ye, lass", she had said on her death bed, "for ye're neither fish nor fowl, nor good red herring".

Maisie thought about it now as she pulled a stool in front of the smouldering turf in the wide fireplace and sat, momentarily easing her back. It was certainly true, what Nonie had said - she belonged nowhere. Indeed, she had never felt she belonged in the Settlement, but she had come to understand that she would not have survived the famine if she had not been fostered here with the childless couple who, along with eleven other families, had opted to 'jump', as it became known, and change to the religion that was preached by Rights by Conscience in return for being fed and housed, after the great hunger had come to Mayo.

The 'jumpers' were shunned by the Catholics who survived, but the Settlement lasted for twenty years until 1876, when famine no longer stalked the land, by which time most of the original inhabitants had either died or returned to the religion and place from where they had come.

The McBrides had stayed on until they died and Maisie had stayed on after that. She had nowhere to return to and she had only known the religion of Pastor Ian Jones, so she lived in isolation, tending her goats and her fowl and her garden and cutting her own turf from the Society's bog nearby.

The Settlement was many miles from the nearest town and the track that connected it to the outside world was overgrown now and nearly impassable. No strangers came that way. She sometimes thought she might lose the power of speech altogether and, except for the songs she sang as she worked, her voice might well have grown rusty.

Now she threw a few sods on the fire to keep it alight while she went to gather limpets on the shore - another task that promised further backache. If she wasn't so tall, she thought, standing up and stretching…She was as tall as the doorway and, in spite of the hardship of her life-style, she had the wild beauty of the stormy coast. Only there was no one to tell her so.

No one - until that moment.

As she stepped out of the door, she saw a black-clad figure coming down the overgrown track. In one hand he carried a stout stick and in the other some kind of bag. She went as far as the gate, staring in amazement, which gave way to anxiety as she saw that the stranger wore the clothing of a priest. Was he coming to turn her out, to re-claim the Settlement for the Catholics? She thought to run, but it was too late. The man in black hailed her. "Is this the Protestant Settlement?"

She made no answer, and he drew closer, finally letting down his bag on the street and repeating the question.

"You can see for yourself it's deserted", she said defiantly, ready to retreat back inside the house. "There's nobody here practicing any religion, but this house in mine". She spoke with a bravado she was far from feeling.

"Thanks be to God"! was the surprising rejoinder. "May I intrude on your hospitality a while"?

Maisie backed up towards her house, her nervousness not allayed by the stranger's odd exclamation and request - a visit from a priest could only mean trouble. But what could she do? "I - I suppose so", she muttered, as she reached the door. "Come in, then".

The man picked up his bag and followed her in, Maisie stood by the hearth, but her visitor flopped down onto a bench by the wall. She saw now that his clothes were torn and muddy, as though he had come along way. He was young and yet his bearded face looked haggard beneath the black hat. "You are going far"? she asked in a low voice.

She was startled anew when he suddenly straightened up. "Perhaps not", he said. "You see…" and with those words he ripped the white collar from his neck. "I am not what I seem", he declared. "I am no priest, but a Bible teacher from the Protestant school at Ballynohone. The village people stormed it and I made my escape disguised like this".

At once contrite, she poured him a cup of milk. "You're famished entirely", she said. "Here it is safe - no one comes by anymore since the pastor left".

With a sigh of relief, he began to sip the milk. He loosened his coat and took off his hat, releasing a fall of hair as black as were the girl's own springy curls. After a while he put down the cup and seemed lost in thought for many moments. Then, "My name is Gilbert Swan". he said quietly. "Would you have me for a neighbour"?

Maisie thought quickly. She was not averse to the idea of company. After a brief pause, she held out her hand. "Maisie O'Hara, and I wouldn't mind a neighbour, at all".

The last cottage to be evacuated was two doors away and had belonged to the O'Tooles. Its condition was not too bad and they set about preparing it and lighting a fire in the hearth. While the newcomer swept and cleaned, Maisie gathered armfuls of bracken to lay on the bed. "It's soft and sweet-smelling", she said, "and I've a blanket or two to spare".

"I'm blest", said Gilbert Swan simply.

Later they supped on rabbit stew with herbs and vegetables from Maisie's garden and afterwards talked long into the night. Maisie telling of her life in the Settlement, with the reluctant converts, and Gilbert telling of his life in Wales as a teacher and, more recently, in the school across the mountains from which he had escaped.

In the ensuing days he made his little house more habitable and learned from Maisie the skills of husbandry. Each grew more and more to enjoy the companionship of the other and inevitably the day came when Gilbert asked his neighbour would she become his wife.

"I don't see how", she responded. "Who'd marry us? We cannot draw down the attentions of the Catholics".

Her reasoning seemed unanswerable.

But in a few days Gilbert found the answer. "We'll join them", he said. "We'll convert the other way and there'll be no more reason to hide".

Maisie agreed. After all, it was the faith of her own people. The year was 1880.

There are still Swans in that corner of the West, but only silence meets enquiries into the past. Nothing remains of the Settlement and "jumpers" is a dirty word.

GOOSE GIRL

————

Sally Devlin ran desperately down the stony hillside, scanning the terrain ahead of her for any sign of her three wayward charges.

In the short time it had taken her to gather some cress from the mountain stream the gander and his two ladies had completely vanished. Worth five, or even ten, shillings each, the birds were an asset the family could ill afford to loose.

Still without a sighting, she plunged into the copse that fringed the no-go area of Squire Bradley's estate. Trespassers man or beast, got short shrift from McCrae, the notorious Scottish land agent. But, bursting out of a thicket, she saw that she was too late - lying on the ground in a sprawl of feathers were her three lovely birds. Beside them, his mouth full of down and dripping with blood, crouched the agent's dog, a misshapen brute, which she later learned was a blood hound. Leaning on his gun behind the scene of carnage was the dreaded Fergus McCrae himself, a smirk on his arrogant face.

Uttering a cry of anguish, Sally lunged towards him, caution thrown to the winds, intent only to avenge her charges.

But she was brought up short. With bared teeth and a rumbling growl, the ugly dog sprang between them. "Down, Sergeant"! commanded his master and the dog backed off as McCrae seized her arm.

She was a strong girl and she wrenched herself free, at the same time letting fly with her other hand to administer a stinging slap on the agent's cheek. "How dare you kill them"! she panted. "You're a thief and a murderer"!

RAGE

The two protagonists glared at each other, the man's dark looks accented by the rage in his eyes, the girl's colour heightened to vie with the copper hair falling around her face. McCrae spoke first. "Get off this land," he said, "and let neither you nor you stock cross its borders again, or the law will deal with you."

Sally flung round and made off back the way she had come. She knew she had passed all limits of sanity and that "law" meant execution in McCrae's vocabulary. In her heart fear quickly replaced anger and she realised it was her own carelessness that had lost the geese.

It was hard going home. She had to admit her negligence - twenty two should be a responsible age.

She told of the slaughter of the geese by the agent's big ugly dog, but she left out her own reaction to spare the family the fear of reprisal - of eviction, perhaps. Her feeling of guilt was overwhelming: the geese were her mother's pride and joy and nothing she could do would compensate for their loss. Hatred grew in her heart for Fergus McCrae.

Then one morning a clatter of hooves on the mountain path announced the approach of a rider. Sally and her mother and young brother, Brian, crowded to the door as the horseman drew up. One look and Sally's heart gave a lurch - it was the hated agent and she felt the worst was upon them.

"You there"! He looked directly at her. "Have you seen my dog, Sergeant? If harm has come to him at your hands, by God, you'll live to regret it"!

"No, Sir, we've seen no dog here, only Bob, our old sheepdog." Kate Devlin was abject in her protestations, but McCrae continued to glare at Sally.

"I've not laid an eye on your ugly dog since we last met"! she blurted out, unable to control her tongue as her hatred surfaced. Then she waited for the consequences, as her mother cringed. But the agent spurred his horse and clattered away.

The little group went back inside. Sally was still seething, but now she had to put up with the nervous reaction of others. "How could you speak up so to himself?" wailed her mother. "It will bring misfortune on us, surely."

"If he doesn't find his dog, the blame will be on us, no doubt." Brian contributed his own fears. Sally said nothing. Once again her temper had got the better of her and her family stood to suffer.

The day passed in uneasy speculation. Towards evening Mick, the man of the house, came up the path from the bog, the creels on the donkey he led loaded with turf. Across the back of the animal and supported by the creels lay the body of a golden brown dog. A shout brought the family to the door of the cottage. "Mother of God - what have you there?" gasped Kate.

But Sally recognised the seemingly - lifeless form. "Tis Sergeant," she whispered. "The devil-god of McCrae."

"Give us a hand with him, will ye," urged Mick. "Tis badly injured he is." Father and son lifted down the unprotesting animal and carried him inside. The dog whimpered as he was set down and it could be seen that one of his front paws was half-severed. "He was caught in a trap," said Mick, "and he was there for some days by the looks of him". He was told of the agent's visit and said young Brian should go and tell McCrae.

"But no," said Sally quickly. "He'll surely think that I am responsible if we inform him so soon after he came looking. I'll tend to his foot and after a while we'll take him back."

In spite of her terrible experience with the dog and the way he had gone for her, Sally's heart contracted with pity as she examined the wound. "Poor Sergeant," she murmured, stroking his floppy ears, and the animal feebly licked her hand. She got water and healing herbs and rags together and she bathed the foot and bandaged it and held his head while he slowly lapped warm milk. They fixed him on a blanket by the hearth for the night and he appeared content enough.

In the morning he was stronger and lapped eagerly at a bowl of bread and milk. When the sun was up, he limped outside, but became uneasy if Sally was gone from his sight. Some strange bond seemed to have developed between them.

She continued to bathe and dress the paw and in a few days the dog could leave his weight upon it and was sharing Bob's dinner of potatoes and buttermilk. He and Sally had become inseparable.

Then Mick brought news from the she-been. "It seems McCrae is offering ten pounds reward for the dog," he related. "A blood hound, it is, and fierce valuable, so 'tis said."

Sally made up her mind. The ten pounds would make up for the geese. With interest! "I'll take him back, so," she said. "His wound has healed up now and I'll not be blamed."

The following morning she tied a rope round Sergeant's neck and the two of them set off for the land agent's house. It was an ivy-covered, two storeyed building in the Bradford demesne, not far from the big house. Sally and the dog walked up the drive and she knocked at the door.

It was opened by a woman Sally knew to be the housekeeper. She gasped when she saw the dog. "Thanks be to God"! she exclaimed. "You have the master's treasure." She leaned forward to take the rope, but Sergeant edged away from her and retreated behind the girl.

"Please to get Mr. McCrae," said Sally. "I would deal with him myself."

Huffed, the housekeeper withdrew and Sally waited.

Soon hurried footsteps announced the agent's approach. When he saw who awaited him, he stopped abruptly. "You"! he said. "You had him all the time. I knew it! There'll be a price to pay for this."

GROWL

Then he, too, made to catch the rope. This time the dog reacted with a snarl and made to bite his erstwhile master's hand. McCrae snatched his hand away and Sally spoke. "My father found your dog in a trap. I nursed him back to health and now I'll thank you for the promised reward."

"Reward, is it"! The agent was furious. "The police will see to you"!

Sergeant gave another menacing growl and it was Sally's turn to say, "Down, Sergeant"!

At that moment the gruff Scottish land agent realised he had met his match in this red-haired mountain lass.

Their eyes met and something ignited between them. He went back into the house and returned shortly after with a ten pound note. Sally took it and in return put the blood hound's rope into his hand and now the dog went to him willingly. Suddenly he smiled and Sally's bitter foe became transformed. "I wouldn't be surprised if Sergeant took to calling on you from time to time," he said.

"Well, to be sure, he'd be very welcome." she replied, and once again the colour in her cheeks began to vie with her copper-coloured hair.

THIEF IN THE NIGHT

———

"BAD CESS TO THE VARMINT"! THE LOUD, VENOMOUS EXCLAMATION ROUSED THE YOUNG BRIDE AND SHE INSTINCTIVELY REACHED FOR HER HUSBAND, ONLY TO REMEMBER, ON ENCOUNTERING NOTHING BUT EMPTY SPACE, THAT THE MEN IN THE HOUSEHOLD WERE AWAY FISHING.

She hurriedly got out of bed. Whatever had enraged her mother-in-law, it did not bode well for the day ahead. Cathy could only hope it was not due to some shortcoming of her own. Nervously she opened the room door. Bridget Clancy stood at the kitchen table, a handful of grey speckled feathers spilling out between her fingers. "May the divil roast his guts"! She glared at the girl, as if she was indeed to blame, her screwed up eyes and wild-looking hair giving her every appearance of a witch, about to perform some hideous rite. She shook the feathers in Cathy's direction. "There goes another of me little flock," she raved. "And her about to get broody, too!"

Cathy cringed. She knew this was a terrible tragedy and that her flock of chickens was Bridget's pride and joy. This was the third in as many weeks that the fox had stolen. "I'll kill him!" she declared. "I'll follow him and I'll block up his hole." She really had no thought but to escape the old woman's wrath and she ran out quickly and headed inland towards the wooded area, where the fox was surely holed up somewhere.

*****

As she ran over the grass and began to mount the hillside, she noticed the odd feather, shed by the marauder's prey, as he carried her back to the den.

If only she could in some way revenge the killing, she thought, it might make her more acceptable to her mother-in-law, with whom relations had not been easy since Paddy Joe had wed her. She had not brought much of a bride price and his parents had been reluctant to accept the orphan from Inishkeen, the island from where he and his father based their fishing trips. But love had prevailed and they had to make do with the few sheep that were all her uncle could muster.

Her thoughts were interrupted by the sound of a horn, followed by the baying of hounds and shortly afterwards a line of horses appeared, galloping in pursuit of the dogs as they passed above her at the edge of the trees. The Manor hounds, she realised. Please God they would catch the thieving fox. She slowed her pace, but continued on in the hope of finding evidence of their success.

After a while she gained the trees. The hunt was long out of sight and sound, but her desire for acceptance by the Clancy's urged her on. The trees, she found, consisted merely of a narrow belt and she was soon through them. The hunt could only have borne to the left to skirt a steep escarpment and she carried on in its wake.

Someway along, a rough track became visible, apparently ending at an overgrown quarry. Cathy paused at the edge of what had become a considerable crater, perhaps caused by a rockfall after it had been abandoned. She thought she heard the huntsman's horn faintly in the distance.

Then, as though in reply, a bark came from below the tangled bushes at her feet - a bark that petered out in a high-pitched whine and a series of yaps. Cathy peered through the vegetation, but could see nothing. However, the sound had been full of panic; there was a suffering animal down there. Could it be the fox, she wondered, chased over the rim by the hounds - perhaps wounded? This might be her chance to finish it off.

Cautiously she began to clamber down, slipping and sliding and clutching the bushes as stones loosened beneath her feet. Eventually, with a final slither, she landed on a pile of rubble. Looking round, as she gained her balance, she prepared to confront an injured fox and tried to identify a suitable rock to use as a weapon.

Nothing moved.

Then another high-pitched yap. It seemed to come from behind a boulder across where she stood. Selecting a large stone, she took hold of it and crept towards the sound. Arriving in front of the boulder, she straightened up and peered over the top. Lying wedged between it and the bank was a foxhound. She knew this from having seen pictures of them in an English magazine and realised at once that it must have been part of the pack that had so recently passed that way.

She dropped her weapon and leaned over to touch the dog, which immediately started to lick her hand and whine. What to do? The animal seemed to be firmly trapped and maybe injured, but she couldn't possibly leave it there. She tried to move the boulder, but could make no impression.

Eventually she clambered round to the back of it and, making soothing noises to the dog, she squirmed down beside it, got her feet against the stone and pushed with all her strength. With a wobble and then a sudden jerk, it rolled away, leaving her self and the dog in a tangled heap behind it.

She picked herself up and encouraged the animal to do the same, but after a small struggle, it continued to lie there, whimpering. Cathy examined it. She concluded one of its paws was the tenderest spot and that it had probably been wrenched in the fall. How on earth was she to get it out of the quarry?

*****

Finally she managed to pick the whimpering creature up and tuck it under her arm, but the weight was too much for her to be able to keep her balance on the climb up. Then with sudden inspiration, she heaved the body up so that it lay across her shoulders and this seemed manageable.

She pulled her way to the top, bush by bush, the dog lying quietly and occasionally licking her ear. They reached the rim and she collapsed on the ground, the dog on top of her. "What now"? she enquired of it. "It wouldn't be right at all to leave you here."

The dog's tail wagged in agreement.

Cathy surveyed the countryside, all new to her. Presumably that was the Manor house away down in more trees. The hound must belong there. All thoughts of the fox forgotten, she faced into this new problem. Could she carry the heavy dog so far? She supposed she'd have to try. "Come on, then," she encouraged it, once more struggling to heave it up. Balance obtained she began the tricky descent, steadying her burden with a hand on its flank.

Before long, her shoulders began to ache and there was blood on her legs from the scratches of the bushes in the quarry. She began to doubt if she could reach the Manor.

She had, however, got to the fringe of the trees when a horseman appeared. They spotted each other simultaneously and the rider rapidly approached and reined in at her side. "What's this"? he demanded, sliding to the ground. "I declare it's Ranger! He's been missing since the hunt." He lifted the dog from Cathy's shoulders and set it on the ground, to which it sank with a whimper.

"He's hurt, Sir," said Cathy. "He fell into a quarry and was trapped under a rock. I found him when I was following the fox and I carried him out."

The rider's eyes traveled over the girl's weary appearance and torn legs and he found it hard to believe such a slight lass had borne the heavy dog so far. "You must return with me to the Manor," he then said. "Squire Grant will be grateful to you for saving his favourite hound." He pulled his horse around and lifted the dog up in front of the saddle. Then he mounted himself. "Let you stand on that hillock," he directed Cathy, "and climb up behind me."

Nervously she did as she was bid, for never in her life had she been so near a horse before. But she clambered up and put her arms around the stranger's waist. Then, slowly and carefully, they proceeded downwards through the trees, finally joining the driveway to the big house.

As they approached the imposing building, Cathy caught her breath. It was like a dream to the girl from an island cabin to find herself riding up to the Squire's house. But they skirted the building and went round to the back. Here the huntsman, for it was he, dismounted, helped Cathy down and, with the dog in his arms, led the way through the back door and into the vast kitchen, where an elderly woman came forward. The situation was explained to her. "Have the Master told that his dog is safe," concluded the narrator," and have the young lady's cuts attended to."

Amid the ensuing flurry of activity, Cathy found her legs begin bathed, a bowl of stew set in front of her and finally a summons from the Squire himself. This elderly, bearded gentleman regarded her kindly and asked her to repeat her story of finding the dog. She did so again, explaining her reason for going after the fox.

"You're a brave lass," said the Squire at the end of her tale, "and you shall have a hen and her chicks to take back home with you."

At that point, Cathy was absolutely sure that she was dreaming. And the dream lasted all the way back to the Clancy's cottage in the pony trap driven by the stable boy and accompanied by a large box containing a mother hen and her thirteen chicks and elated by the news that the fox had been caught and killed by the hounds.

The sound of the trap brought Bridget to the door and she stared in amazement as Cathy alighted from it with the boy behind her, carrying the box. The girl spoke first. "I've good news," she said. The fox is dead, and look, the lost birds are replaced." She opened a corner of the box and the old woman peered in. "Well, God is good," she exclaimed, "to have blessed me with such a daughter-in-law!"

Cathy laughed and hoped she would never wake up from this dream.

BOYS FOREVER

———

To the casual observer it would not have been apparent that Pat O'Flynn was still a boy. He had the lined, weather-beaten face and stiffening body of a man well over fifty. Only those resident in the west of Ireland and acquainted with the isolated village in the mountains where the family lived would be aware of his Peter Pan qualities. Pat remained young because he was a bachelor. The moment he married he would cease to be a boy, but in the words of the song, he might be one for years, or it might be forever.

According to the statistics of the time, sixty-two per cent of all males in Ireland between the ages of thirty and thirty-five were unmarried, and three out of every four to reach fifty remained bachelors. It was not that people like Pat had an unnatural taste for celibacy, but that they were simply unable to find a way of escape from a system based on the economic pattern of rural life.

Pat's family consisted of father and mother, himself, a sister and two brothers. Their farmhouse formed part of a small community tucked away in the Connermara mountains and barely accessible by road. The holding of fifteen acres was described as 'the place of four cows and a horse', and they worked it between them. The father was owner, director and principal worker. The sons were his 'boys', subordinate to him in everything - a situation that would persist until such time as one married, when the farm would be made over to him.

But which one would that be? Free-will did not come into the question, because this decision also rested with the father. Although Pat was the eldest of the boys, this was no indication that he would be the heir; the farmer had full power to choose among his sons, all having equal status. Before the famine all sons and daughters could hope to be settled on the land, but since then holdings could not be sub-divided, so only one son could inherit.

When the father felt old age - sometimes extreme old age - creeping up on him, he would announce that the time had come for him to retire and would immediately set about selecting a suitable spouse for the chosen son. As this step, however, involved a crucial reorganization, the old couple would put it off as long as possible.

In the case of the O'Flynn family, Pat's two brothers had given up hope and emigrated, so they were out of the picture. His sister was married into a business family in the local town, where the urban situation was not a great deal different. The town was linked closely to the rural hinterland, on which it depended for its life-blood. Custom decreed that the bride of a shopkeeper-to-be must be a country girl, because his entire future trade depended on whom he married, the family and friends of his wife considering it an obligation to buy from him. Pat was the natural heir. However, the father's reluctance to sign the place over simply became too prolonged - he died without having done so. This left Pat completely without status; the farm was not his and he had no legal rights or jurisdiction over anything on the land or premises. He would never now become adult and be able to take his place at the hearth seat when visiting, be among the first group to come forward at Mass, or to give his opinion wherever local groups might form. As a boy, he would have to continue to gather with the other boys in a particular place where they laughed and joked and played cards, instead of joining the men, where local problems were settled and matters relating to farming decided. They were the ones who had 'a responsibility on them', and who influenced and integrated the community.

Obviously Pat could not emigrate like his brothers; someone had to look after the farm and the ageing mother. If only he had gotten married, everything would have been different. As it was, he would be an unacceptable husband and no bride price would be coming into the place to make necessary improvements.

Eventually the old mother died and Pat was on his own. For a boy of the rural west this was a bleak situation. But girls, too, could find themselves in a similar position, especially if it had been the obligation of an only daughter to stay at home to tend elderly parents. On their death she would be too old and inexperienced either for marriage or to seek fresh pastures. Without even the camaraderie that the boys enjoyed, an isolated spinster would become a virtual hermit.

Such a girl lived up a boreen past Pat O'Flynn's house at the end of the glen. They rarely encountered one another and when they did, were too reserved to embark on a conversation. If one said "A grand day, thank God,' the only reply would be, "It is, surely." And yet, would not a pairing of these two mean the elimination of the terrible burden of loneliness, which each must share in isolation, and seem like a natural development?

It was not an option either of them considered. Then nature decided to take a hand. At the back end of a dreary winter there came a day of wind and rain the like of which could not later be recollected by even the oldest members of the community. All day long and into the night the wind shrieked and the rain cascaded down until it seemed as if the mountain would melt away. and that is, in fact, what happened, it was going on for three in the morning. Pat was still crouched by the hearth, trying to keep a bit of a blaze going, as sleep would have been out of the question, when a thump came at the door, followed by a wild crying that mingled with, and yet was not quite part of, the wind's unearthly din.

Startled and not a little afraid, he got to his feet and listened again. Another thump came, another wail. This time there was no mistaking; someone - or something - was out there in the storm. Full of foreboding, he drew back the bolt and inched the door open, but at the first crack it was pushed violently inwards and an extraordinary apparition fell into the room. Streaming with water and plastered with mud, the almost unrecognisable figure of Mary Glennon from up the boreen staggered, moaning, towards the fire. "Merciful Heaven", said Pat, ramming the door shut behind her. "What in the name of God . . .?" After he had ripped the cover off his bed to dry her and covered her with blankets and given her strong tea, laced with whiskey, she mumbled her terrible story. She told of how the house had begun to tremble and of how a pounding had started on the back of it. As she had cringed in terror, the door had burst open and a river of rocks and mud poured through. She had barely been able to get out through the front before being overwhelmed. She did not know how long it had taken to slide and roll down the mountain side through the fury of the storm before reaching his house. "And my home has gone now", she sobbed at the end. "What'll I do, at all?"

In the time it had taken Mary to tell of her misfortune, Pat felt he had become an adult. He was finally responsible for another human being, and it was up to him to make decisions for the future. Filling up her cup again, he patted his visitor reassuringly. "Let you not be worrying yourself", he said firmly. "Isn't this house of mine well able to hold the two of us?"

DEIRBHLE'S CHURCH

THE CRIPPLED GIRL DRAGGED HERSELF PAINFULLY ACROSS THE ROCKS TOWARDS THE RUINED CHURCH. IT HAD ALREADY TAKEN HER HALF THE DAY TO COME THIS FAR FROM THE COTTAGE ON THE TIP OF THE MULLET PENINSULA IN NORTH WEST MAYO.

The year was 1588 and she had managed to eke out a solitary existence since her father and brothers had perished at the hands of Sir Richard Bingham during the Burke rebellion of 1586.

The Mullet was bleak territory, only accessible by sea, with fishing and farming and the occasional plundering of a passing ship the only means of subsistence, and they were not occupations suited to a girl - even a normal one.

But Deirbhle Burke had one leg shorter than another and movement was difficult for her. However, after her mother's death, the burden of the household had fallen on her seventeen year-old shoulders and it had seemed that nothing more was in store for her. Although a beauty by any standards, no man on the Mullet could afford a wife who was less than fit.

Now she had reached the end of her resources and had barely the strength left to crawl to the church of her namesake and petition the saint for aid.

"Blessed Saint Deirbhle, help me", the girl moaned as she struggled on. A miracle was needed, but everyone knew that the saint could perform those. She thought of how a royal princess had come there in the fifth century to renounce the world. When a suitor pursued her, imploring her for a glance from her beautiful eyes, she gouged them out and flung them from her. Where they fell, a spring gushed forth and when she later bathed the sockets therein, her sight was restored and over the centuries pilgrims had flocked to her shrine.

At last she reached the crumbling walls of the church and collapsed inside the sanctuary, her strength completely spent. Over the years wild ferns had colonized the sheltered space, so as Deirbhle sank down beneath her ragged cloak, her red curls in tumbled profusion, she failed to see the recumbent form that lay against the opposite wall.

Meanwhile, unknown to her, the Spanish Armada was being buffeted by storms along the coast and alarming the Government, which expected the ships to land their forces and invade the country. The dreaded Bingham had therefore issued a proclamation ordering "all men to deliver up any Spaniards they encountered or to face the penalty of death".

Two days previously the Santa Anna had run aground nearby and all aboard had hastily disembarked, but had pretty soon run foul of a contingent of soldiers and had scattered in all directions.

After plunging through bogs and over sand dunes, one of their company had chanced upon the little church and there he had since lain concealed. On seeing the disheveled figure of the girl as she dragged herself in, he concluded she was no threat. He lay still and waited.

After a little while strength returned to Deirbhle and she began to pray to her namesake: "Blessed Lady, I sorely need your help. Succour me. Succour me". With that she felt a hand on her shoulder, causing her to turn round quickly and sit up in shock. She saw a dark, bearded man bending over her in torn and muddy clothes - clothes, all the same, that were those of a nobleman. "Have no fear". He spoke in English with a strange accent.

Deirbhle herself spoke little English, as Gaelic was her native tongue. Nonetheless, she knew the language slightly and she sensed that this man who no enemy. "Who are you"? she said.

The Spaniard straightened up and bowed: "I am Don Pedro de Media of Cadiz", he announced. "I am shipwrecked - the English soldiers pursue me'.

"I am Deirbhle Burke", the girl told him.

"Ah". There was a flash of white teeth. "We go to your house, perhaps?" Deirbhle thought. Her cottage would be safe enough, but she was so weak from hunger. And her leg …. "I don't know", she stammered "Food…."

"Food". The stranger repeated the word. Then, leaning into the ferns, he pulled out a canvas bag. "Ship's rations". He sat beside her and offered bread and salted meat. It seemed like an answer to a prayer. She ate. And thought.

Thoughts which the Spaniard broke into. "A boat?" he asked. "You have a boat? We could sail to safety - to a Spanish ship. To Spain!"

She looked up, her eyes suddenly alight with hope. "My father's boat - yes. We could sail to Clare Island, the stronghold of Granuaille. Then, if we had money …. Spain, maybe".

"Granuaille. Yes. All Spain knows of her. We go …" He stood and held his hand towards her.

But she shook her head. "Without money - no". The pirate queen's exploits were legendary - as was her mercenary character.

"Money? Gold?" Don Pedro tipped up the canvas bag at Deirbhle's feet. She gasped in astonishment as a cascade of gold coins and jewels tumbled out. "Enough?" He spread his hands. Then he picked up a sparkling tiara and placed it on her wind-blown curls. "For you - my Irish senorita!"

Suddenly everything seemed possible. But then … "My leg". She pointed down. "Walking - no".

"What? You are hurt?" The tall man knelt down and touched her bare, scratched feet.

"No! See". She stretched her legs and indicated the short one. "Ah". Understanding dawned in the dark eyes. "No matter. In Spain, special shoe. Make same as other". Scooping up the coins and jewels, he slung the bag over his shoulder and pulled her up, supporting her so as she could limp alongside.

Together they stepped outside and came to the holy well. Here Deirbhle pulled her companion to a halt. She took the jewel-encrusted tiara from her head and dropped it into the clear water. "For saving my life", she said, and the Spaniard nodded.

In turn he lifted a gold cross from about his neck and threw it after. "From me, also", he murmured. "In thanks for my beautiful saviour".

They met with no trouble on the journey back to the cottage and dawn was breaking as Deirbhle opened the door. She pointed up to the loft where the sails and oars of the boat had lain since her men had gone and Don Pedro manoeuvred them down. With the aid of a stick, she limped ahead of him to where the boat lay beside a pier.

Then she watched as it was prepared for sea. She had no doubts that their voyage would be successful. Wasn't the blessed saint taking care of them?

The Spaniard looked up and called to her as the sail flapped in the breeze. He stepped ashore and lifted her aboard and they were away. As the land receded, Deirbhle felt no sorrow: the Mullet had given her a harsh life. She met the eyes of the Spaniard and suddenly they laughed together and the sound held all the rich warmth of the Mediterranean sun.

THE CITY BOY

————

MARY KATE DAN PULLED STRONGLY AGAINST THE INCOMING TIDE, THE MUSCLES IN HER ARMS FLEXING AND RELAXING IN CO-ORDINATION WITH THE STROKES OF THE OARS.

She was well used to the passage between the shore and the island, she being, as it were, the only link in the family chain connecting her aunt and uncle to the new generation **of** emigrants on the mainland and beyond. The last of the once-flourishing Inishreen community, Mick and Bridget Garavan had resisted all efforts to transfer them to a more convenient home, preferring to end their days in familiar territory.

Mary Kate did not know how the old pair would receive the news she was bringing them, the news that their brother Willie's son from Birmingham had decided to pay them a visit before facing into the arduous responsibilities of adult life.

Indeed, their reaction was as she expected. After beaching the boat, she had made her way along the shore and up the steps to the cottage, where Mick was waiting at the door, having seen her approach. "What brings you across on a Saturday,

Mary Kate?" he enquired suspiciously. Isn't this the day you go to the town for supplies?"

"It would be, Uncle, in the normal way of things," she told him, "only I have some special news for you today."

"And what might that be?" Good news was not to be expected at their time of life and he braced himself for the worst.

"It's Willie Pat's son, Tom." His niece decided to take the bull by the horns. "He's coming to visit you."

"What's that? What are you saying?" The old man stepped back into the kitchen as though needing his sister's support. "That's a city boy. What business would he have with the likes of us?"

Mary Kate followed him in, trying to calm him down. "Well, it's only natural, isn't it, that he'd want to see his father's place, meet his relations.." a screech from her aunt silenced her. "I'll have no city boy here! Laughing at us, he'd be, and him used to grand foreign ways"! She banged the pot oven down on the floor and stood with her hands on her hips, defying Kate to best her.

Mary Kate glanced out of the window. "Faith and it's little use your objections are now", she exclaimed. "Tis on the way he is. Martin Ruane's boat has just pushed off from beyond and he has a passenger with him!"

The brother and sister rushed out of the door and peered across the bay. "The Lord save us"! Old Bridget crossed herself piously. "I must be readying the room . ." She disappeared behind them in an outraged fluster, while Mick and the younger woman continued to gaze at the approaching vessel.

"It's a poor thing when we can't be left in peace." The grumbles continued. "And the cow due for calving and all; sure we've no time to be entertaining his like."

"Ah, don't be taking on so". Mary Kate was becoming a little irritated. "You've no nature in you . . it's a wonder you'd not be glad to see Willie Pat's boy." She herself was anticipating the encounter with pleasure.

But the old man was not to be mollified. "Willie Pat, is it?" he growled. "Willie Pat, who never set foot in the place since he left it forty years since! So what brings this young spalpeen now?"

Mary Kate wished she knew. But whatever the reason, it was bound to liven up the summer months ahead. Not that she would have time for any playacting herself; she had her hands full with the care of her parents and the tending of their few acres in Glynn - a poor substitute, she had always thought, for the island land, although her father's share of it had not amounted to a great deal . . it was Uncle Mick, as acknowledged king of Inishreen, who had claimed the best portion. Martin Ruane's boat drew closer and his passenger became more clearly defined. He seemed to be of small stature and to have little or no hair. Mary Kate had noted this fashion among young people she had seen on television - it was not, she thought, attractive. Her uncle was of a like mind. "He's a quare-looking bosthune", he muttered. "May the divil take Willie Pat for sending him!"

Mary Kate left him to his grumbling and went slowly down to the landing strip to wait for the boat to pull in. As sturdy as the visitor was slight, the bloom of health that radiated from her and her abundant chestnut hair was in even greater contrast to the paleness and pinched features of the city boy. In a few moments the keel grounded on the rocks and Martin Ruane steadied his passenger as he stepped ashore to grasp the out-stretched hand of his cousin. "You're welcome to Inishreen, Tom", she said. "It's tired you'll be after the journey, so come on up to the house". The boatman handed out the traveller's bag and with a salutation to the girl and a wave towards the house, he pushed off again and settled in to the oars.

Tom stood looking around him with a bewildered air. "This is it, then?" he said in a Birmingham accent. "Small, isn't it - and desolate like?" He hunched his shoulders, making them look even narrower beneath the leather jacket he was wearing.

Mary Kate smiled, sensing his nervous uncertainty. "It's big enough", she said. "Too big sometimes for them that's in it."

"How many would that be?" His glance took in the vacant houses that stood abandoned along the sea's edge.

"Tis just the two of them in it - Uncle Mick and Aunt Bridget." "Gawd!" he said and the girl laughed at his dismay.

They climbed the steps to the house. The old man had retreated inside and was bending over the fire as they entered. "Here's Tom," Mary Kate introduced him. "Let ye sit down and I'll wet the tea." Mick held out his hand reluctantly. "You're welcome," he said, seating himself at the table and nodding at Tom to do likewise. "You'll not be getting much comfort here," he continued. "it's far from the city we are."

The door to the room opened and Bridget came through. She stood and surveyed the visitor. "Faith, then, it's not your father you took after", she remarked, "Willie Pat was aye a big strong lad."

"I'm still growing", Tom smirked defensively. "I'll be as big as me Da yet".

"Hm!" Scorn showed on both the old faces, but Mary Kate brought a measure of harmony to the table as she bustled about pouring the tea and cutting slices of fresh soda bread. "Why wouldn't you, Tom?" she soothed him. "Weren't all the island men big, and you'll be no different."

The young man still looked uneasy and as if he couldn't believe where he'd landed. "What's there to do here, then?" he asked.

"Do!" Mick answered him. "There's work - that's what to do. And you'll be finding out, it you intend to stay."

Mary Kate felt sorry for her cousin, although she knew that the old couple's bark was worse that their bite. "Let him be", she said. "He'll soon settle in. I'll be leaving him to you now." She finished her tea and stood up. "The tide is turning and I must be away."

Tom looked up, shocked. "You're leaving?" he said.

"Yes. Sure, I don't live here at all. I live across on the mainland. Be seeing you . . ." She left the three of them round the table and went back to her boat, wondering what would be the outcome of this unexpected visit.

Her parents waited eagerly for news of the visitor, laughing heartily when she described her cousin. "You'll see Mick landing the lad out again tomorrow", prophesied her father, Dan.

But no such sight was seen and Mary Kate was kept so busy on the holding that it was some days before she found time to make another trip to the island. "Where's Tom, then?" she asked on arrival, no sign of him being visible in the cottage.

Her uncle looked into the fire with studied indifference.

"Fishing", he said.

"Fishing! Alone?" She was aghast. "But . . "

"He was awful sick at first". The old man laughed at the memory. "But he's a fast learner". at that moment Tom came in the door. His leather jacket had been replaced by an old jersey of Mick's, his face had lost that pinched look; two mackerel swung from his hand. On seeing Mary Kate he grinned cheekily. "Am I growing?" he asked, stretching out his arms in the baggy jersey.

Surprise making her uncertain how to respond, the girl stared at him until Bridget pushed her way by and took hold of the fish. "You'll have the sup with us?" turning to Mary Kate.

"I will so". She could still hardly believe Tom's new confidence, but over the tea she found her tongue and the chat flowed freely between them.

Over the weeks ahead Tom's confidence grew - as did his hair, until it matched Mary Kate's own in luxuriant chestnut growth. By the end of the summer he was a proficient oarsman and the old couple on the island had come to depend on him.

So it was a sorry day that he told them he must return to Birmingham.

"I'll be back, though", he promised. But in spite of this assertion, Mick and Bridget were as put out by his departure as they had been by his arrival. For Mary Kate, too, a light had been extinguished and the winter loomed ahead, dark and cheerless.

But an unimaginable surprise was in store for all of them.

It was the beginning of October, Mary Kate was on the island, unloading stores from the boat, when the old man gave a shout. "Martin Ruane's coming and he has passengers with him!"

She dropped everything and ran up the steps to see better. "Who can it be?" she wondered.

"It looks uncommon like Tom. But the other . . ." He scratched his head in perplexity.

Hurriedly putting away the shopping, they waited for the boat to land.

"It's Tom, all right", Smiles lit up the old faces and Mary Kate started to wave in welcome. As the boat grounded, Tom jumped out. The cousins hugged. "I brought me Da!" he shouted. "He's come home at last!"

The bags were handed out; the boatman left and the little party made its way to the house. "Tom!" Bridget enveloped the lad in a hug. Then, "It's never Willie Pat!" to the man coming along behind. "None other,' said the newcomer. For some moments they sized each other up. Then a flurry of hand-shakes. And "Welcome homes". And, "Tis long enough you're away." at last they were seated and the inevitable tea was readied. Willie Pat explained his presence. "When the young lad here described the place - the empty houses and all - well it seemed like a good place to come back to and myself in the building trade these many years. I could fix one up, like. Would there be room on the land for us - the wife is dead and there's just the two of us?" "There'd be no trouble there" Mick eyed his brother with bemusement. "But - it's a quiet life after the city . . ."

"I was thinking I might do up a few of the houses . . Perhaps Dan and Mary might like to move back from Glynn. . maybe others".

Mary Kate and Tom looked at each other and under the table they clasped hands.

"And would you be able to rule it like you did before"?

"Hah!" The hesitation vanished. He got to his feet and gripped the sides of the table. "Once a king," he said proudly, "always a king."

THE LAST COASTGUARD

"AND WHERE EXACTLY MIGHT YOUR HUSBAND BE MA'AM?"
THE TALL FIGURE OF THE COASTGUARD DARKENED THE
DOOR OF THE ISLAND COTTAGE, SO THAT THE TWO WOMEN
INSIDE MERGED INTO THE SHADOWS.

The old one answered him, her voice was a feeble mixture
of fear and defiance. "My husband is dead these ten years
sir. There's no cause for you to be troubling myself and my
daughter".

"It's a routine check", the man replied. We've got good
cause to believe that there are guns being landed along this
coast". His gaze took in the dark interior and rested briefly
on the young woman at the hearth, her head bent forward
covering her face with a tumble of black hair. "Good day to
you then", he paused, as if waiting for a response - "for now",
he concluded, as none was forthcoming.

The women listened until they could no longer hear his
footsteps crunching the pebbles on the shore. Then, "What
was he like, mam?" The girl turned sightless eyes towards her
mother as a wistful smile played across her lips. "He didn't
sound harsh - strong, but not harsh".

"Musha!" Scorn filled the old woman's voice. "He's no different to the rest of the English forces. Bad cess to the lot of them!"

Old Maura Flynn had witnessed the building of the coastguard station on Gurteen Point in 1890, which had severely curtailed the smuggling activities of her late husband. This was not the first time she had been visited by the Revenue men, although, of late, their visits had dwindled. She had not seen today's caller before.

"They have to do their duty." Resignation and a certain eagerness crept into the young voice. The occasional forays of the coastguards to the offshore islands had created a diversion for the blind girl; since her father's death they had nothing to hide and none had treated her roughly. She often wished she could see them in their smart uniforms, coming and going in the patrol boat. As she had not recognised the voice of the man who had just left, she thought he might be a newcomer….

"Duty, is it!" Her mother snorted. "Destroying the livelihood of the native people. They'll be welcome on this island over my dead body!"

Looking back on it, it seemed to the blind girl, Catherine, a strangely prophetic utterance. Less than a week later, her mother was dead. It happened after a visit from the Moran brothers from one of the outer islands. They had come at daybreak, their curragh gliding silently onto the pier below the cottage. The knock on the door had wakened her and the hoarse, whispered message had filled her with dread, as it seemed to fill the room. "The Fenians are rising - be ready!"

They were gone as quickly as they had come. But they had galvanised the old woman. She rushed outside after them and regardless of the air of secrecy, which had hung like a shroud about the brothers, began hopping and lepping on the flagstones and shrieking "Erin go Bragh!" at the top of her lungs.

"Stop, mam! Stop will you!" Catherine got hurriedly out of bed. Although blind since the age of nine, her sense of location was acute. In moments she had reached her mother's side. As she grabbed her, the old woman suddenly went limp. With a faint gurgle, she slipped out of her grasp and collapsed on the ground.

"Mam! Mam!" In desperation Catherine bent over her. "What's wrong? Speak to me…" The body of her mother lay inert. She sank down beside her, cradling the silent head in her arms, while tears flowed down her cheeks.

After a while, she got to her feet, stifling her sobs, and tried to lift the still form inside. She failed to hear the approaching footsteps until a hand was laid on her shoulder and a man's voice said, "What's going on here?"

The girls sensitive ears recognised it as the coastguard's, the man who had so lately come to the island, and she half turned towards him. "Help me, please" she gasped. "Something has happened to Mam."

Her burden was taken gently from her and as she went first into the cottage, her mother's words came vividly back to her - "Over my dead body." Could she really be dead? Another sob wracked her, as she felt over the surface of the bed, smoothing the quilt into place. "Lay her down here" she said, and the coastguard did as he was told. Catherine could sense that he was loosening the old woman's clothing and listening for a heartbeat. "I'm afraid she's gone", he said then, straightening up. "I'll notify the authorities." She could feel his eyes on her. "I was out in the boat when I heard shouting. Was anyone here?"

"No, no one." She recovered quickly. The Moran brothers must have heard her mother. If they saw the patrol boat at the pier, they might suspect them of being in collusion with the King's men. "Please go now" she added. "And - thank you."

She did not go with him to the door and was unaware that he had paused on the threshold, regarding her with a puzzled look, as she ran her hands over the body and adjusted the surrounding objects by touch.

He kept his word about informing the priest. The islanders gathered at the Flynn cottage and the funeral rites were enacted. It would be hard for the girl, but she would not go hungry. Fish were regularly brought to her door; if a beast was killed, she got her share, and one boatman or another regularly brought her the few things she needed from the mainland town. With the cow and the poultry she was well able to feed herself - the accidental blow to her head with an oar might have damaged her optic nerve, but her remaining senses had become more finely tuned in compensation. What she felt now was the isolation.

But sometimes her senses told her that she was being observed and this gave her some unease in view of the warning from the Moran brothers that the Fenians were rising. Was she being watched for some purpose? At times a shiver flicked up her spine. The mystery was solved by an accident.

While pursuing an errant calf along the shore one day, she slipped on a patch of seaweed, striking her knee against a jagged rock. She gave a cry of pain and tried to stand again, her leg buckled beneath her and she sank back, moaning, feeling blood beginning to ooze between her fingers as she clutched the injured limb. As she leaned against the offending rock in dismay, a scatter of pebbles from the shore-line bank alerted her to some-one's presence. A crunching of larger stones came next and then she was being lifted up.

Her face was pressed into uniform buttons and serge; she knew immediately who had come to her aid. But no word was said during the journey to the cottage. The coastguard sat her on a chair, bathed her knee and tore a cloth into strips to bind it. "You take too many risks Catherine," he said when the job was finished. "It's not right for you to be here alone." "You know my name," she replied. "But I do not know yours." "My name is Samuel Dowling," he told her. "And I'd be in trouble for visiting you, if it was known. We are forbidden to fraternize with the native people." "Why did you come then?" A sense of danger took hold of her. If it meant trouble for him, it meant as much for her - the coastguards were the enemy. "I was worried for you **w**hen your mother died - I've been watching out for you."

So she had not been wrong when she had felt strange eyes upon her. The feeling of danger veered towards excitement. But, "you'd best go now," she said. "The pain has left my knee - I'll be all right."

The coastguard stood up. She could tell he was a tall man, as well as broad. And he was no youngster; she knew the customs men were all recruited from the navy. They were experienced sailors. He was clean shaven too - his face had brushed against her forehead when he'd picked her up like a child...Now his hand rested momentarily on her own. "I'll be back," he said, and she listened as he walked away.

In the days that followed, she felt less alone. And, indeed, there seemed to be strange comings and goings on the island. The men that called to her with fish and other messages seemed furtive and did not delay, but over and above their visits she waited for the coastguard...

He came one night at dusk. This time he took her hands in his and she could feel the current of urgency that was in him. "Something's brewing," he said.

"We have guns mounted at the station - there's round the clock watch. Take care until I come back again." He pulled her to him and suddenly she was in his arms and his urgent lips were seeking hers. He released her then abruptly and his hands caressed her face. "Take care." he said, and then was gone.

He left her breathless. Her heart was pounding as she steadied herself against the door jamb, listening to the last sounds of his departure. Then listening, listening, long, long after there was nothing to hear but the slop of waves against the stones. Samuel....an enemy of the islanders, between whom and his life was there incessant strife. Only to her among them was he gentle. And only with him had she ever felt such turmoil and excitement as now possessed her. But the threat of death hung heavily in the air. Trouble threatened and it chilled her heart.

That night the sound of shots disturbed her. She longed for, and yet dreaded, to get news. Had the Fenians attacked the coastguards? Had any of the islanders been killed? Either way, it seemed impossible that Samuel would come again. The next day brought news of a skirmish; the coastguards had intercepted an illegally powered boat that was attempting to land. Shots had been fired by both parties, but the smugglers had got away. No-one had been hurt. Yet, thought Catherine, it could only be a matter of time before the situation exploded.

Dread filled her days and nights. She hardly slept. Her days were spent listening - for what, she scarcely knew; for shots, for shouts, for the scrape of a boat landing…. she felt more isolated than ever before.

And then the Moran brothers came again: she recognised their voices before they approached the door. "It's all over." the elder spoke without preamble. "The treaty is signed, we have a free state and the King's men are away!" "Away…" her heart gave a lurch and she grabbed the table for support. "The coastguards have gone then?" "Aye." Seamus Moran gave a short laugh. "When they heard the news, they locked the doors of the station behind them, got into their boats, and left our shores forever." "We came to tell you that you need fear no more visits from them." added his brother. "God be with you now."

They left her then and the cold chill of dispair enveloped her. So, Samuel had gone without a word and she was condemned to wander this lonely island by herself until the end of her days. The tears came finally, falling unheeded from her sightless eyes.

Oblivious to the passing time, she sat on, while the fire died behind her and the night closed in. At last her head sank onto her folded arms and she slept fitfully. She did not hear the step on the flags, or the scrape of a chair, but when she stirred she knew she was no longer alone. "Who is it?" she breathed but in her heart she knew, before her hands were enfolded in the sailor's. "Samuel, they told me all of you had sailed away…" Samuel got up and drew her to him. "Not quite all." he murmured "because one of them decided to stay behind." As Cathy clung to him in the darkness, a light came on inside her that lit up the universe and she knew that eyes were never necessary when you could see with your heart.

THE BIG WIN

"DRAT IT - WHERE'S THAT TICKET"? AT THE SOUND OF THE ELDERLY PRIEST RUMMAGING AROUND, HIS HOUSEKEEPER WOKE UP WITH A START FROM A NAP AND REALISED THAT THE LOTTERY NUMBERS HAD JUST BEEN CALLED OUT.

She saw the ticket on the floor and reached for it. The priest compared it with the numbers he had copied down and gasped, "This is it, Celia. I've won!

The young woman, his niece, got up and stared over his shoulder. She realised immediately that the numbers she was looking at were her own - it was her ticket she had picked up off the floor. "It's I who have won, Father", she said. "That's my ticket".

"Nonsense, child", the priest blustered. "I dropped my ticket by the chair - no doubt about that. It's the will of God - the parish sorely needs the money." He stood up, ready to set the wheels of finance turning . . . and exposed the ticket he had been sitting on. "Excuse me, Father". Celia picked it up and held it out. "This is your ticket. Mine is the winning one."

Her uncle hesitated, his face became mottled and finally he sat down again. "Well, it makes no difference", he muttered. "Its' the parish that will benefit either way."

Celia O'Hora smiled. "We'll see," she said. The smile hovered on her face for the rest of the evening and for most of the night as she reviewed her life to date.

From the time she had been labeled 'backward' at school, any idea of making a life for herself away from the village had been wiped out. Fate had assigned her the role of farm drudge and through her late teens and early twenties she had toiled away at the beck and call of her brother, who was biding his time until the place was signed over to him. It was Father Tom who had rescued her on his return from Australia, when he had been allocated the parish of Maghery as a sop to his declining years. Having checked out the situation on the home farm, he had stated that he needed a housekeeper and that his niece was the obvious choice. Her brother, Martin, could get married and that would solve any domestic problems in that quarter.

The family had resisted, but the priest's word was still law in the remote west and Celia had shaken the mud off her heels with pleasure and gone to a new life sixty miles away. At first her indoor duties had been a welcome change, but as time passed she had come to feel more isolated. She learned that the priest's housekeeper was someone apart from the rest of the community and she was aware that the stigma of 'backward' had followed her from home - probably lent wings by her disgruntled brother, she thought.

She knew she was not stupid, as the word implied, but she had the inability to express things in writing and therefore failed all tests. But the knowledge brought her no solace, because it was not a failing anybody understood - or, indeed, that she felt able to explain, so a gulf remained, that she seemed unable to bridge, between herself and the parishioners. She was as much a prisoner in the priest's house as she had been on the farm.

Marriage was the only possible escape route and, even though the years were passing, she was still comely enough - better, indeed, than in her younger days, now that the rough farm look had worn off. Her red hair was lustrous and it framed a strong face with high cheek bones and well-defined brows that accented hazel eyes. She was tall, too- able for anything; able to give and receive love, but condemned to limbo. Not any more, though, and she laughed softly in the night, thinking of the life that lay ahead.

In the morning she claimed the prize.

By the end of the week there wasn't a soul in the country who didn't know that the priest's housekeeper in the remote parish of Maghery had become a millionairess. Her face had entered the living rooms of the nation's citizens. The 'backward' epithet was a thing of the past.

Then the letters started to come. In two weeks she'd had twenty-five proposals of marriage, plus a sackful of requests for money. She no longer opened them. Her brother and his new wife had visited, saying that she should come home, that there was always a place for her, that the children would need an aunt. The parishioners no longer seemed shy of her, the young men tried to engage her in conversation at the local store and attendance at Mass increased phenomenally, with the churchgoers from other town-lands crowding in with the hope of speaking to, or even seeing, the millionairess.

Suddenly the world was her oyster - but she wasn't quite sure how to open it. She felt like somebody and nobody at the same time; she was someone whom everybody knew, or wanted to know, but it wasn't for herself. So she did nothing, beyond giving Father Tom a cheque for a community hall, and after a while the novelty of having a lotto-winner in their midst wore off (especially one so unapproachable) and the parishioners forgot about her.

She began to feel even more of a prisoner than before; from being worried that no one noticed her, she was afraid to appear in case they were reminded of who she was.

The situation had more or less reverted to pre-win times, apart from her uncle's constant complaints about the disrepair of the church and the house's need for a new roof, when he arrived home one evening, after calling to a sick parishioner, with a stranger in tow. "Prepare the spare room, Celia," he said, all business-like. "We have a visitor from Australia!" Celia jumped to her feet. How extraordinary! Father Tom had never said he was expecting anyone . . . she took in the figure who had followed him into the house - a youngish man, very blonde, very sunburnt, not very well off, judging by his clothes. "It's amazing", the priest started to explain. "I was passing the railway station and he was thumbing a lift, so I stopped and … and". Amazement overcame him, so the visitor continued.

"You see, Miss, I knew Father O'Hora in Queensland and when I heard he'd returned to the old country, I figured to look him up. We might even be related - Horan is near enough to O'Hora…" He held out his hand. "Mick Horan". "You're welcome." Celia's hand was enveloped in a strong brown one and shaken vigorously. She prayed that her uncle would make no mention of her wealthy status, as she hurried upstairs to make ready the room.

Back down in the kitchen, she hastily prepared sandwiches and carried in the tray. Mick Horan moved quickly to take it from her and made sure she was seated before returning to his own chair. The conversation resumed and Australia was the topic. It sounded fascinating, Celia thought. Her uncle had never talked much about it, except to tell her a story once about how he had been lost in the desert and near to dying of thirst, when a ranger had found him and brought him to safety. She suddenly wondered if the visitor had been that ranger. If so, the priest maintained discretion - as he apparently had in her own case. After that first evening, Mick Horan settled in. He seemed to prefer pouring over the priest's collection of old historical books to exploring the countryside, although on a few occasions he borrowed his host's car and invited Celia to accompany him on short tours of the district.

She was always very careful to steer well clear of the O'Hora place - God forbid, she thought, that they would ever encounter any of her money-grabbing family, who would immediately reveal the secret she was trying to preserve. Because, for the first time in her life, she was enjoying the company of somebody - not as a backward menial, and not as a rich woman, either. But as herself.

"Tell me more about Australia," she invariably started their conversations. "Tell me about your work." And Mick would describe his work on a ranch, tell her about the rich pastures and the arid deserts and the native aborigines.

"Tell me about Ireland," he would say in turn. "Tell me about you." (A subject to be avoided as much as possible, she thought.) One day he decided to visit Galway, but Celia was unable to go, as her uncle was expecting a visit from some committee and she had to be there to serve them. "That's a shame," he said. "But would you write a list of all the places I should see there?"

They were alone in the kitchen at the time and Celia felt her face colouring. "I - I wouldn't know", she said quickly. "It'd be best to ask Father. Excuse me…." she hurried from the room and sent the priest in to the mystified young man.

"Ah, Celia wouldn't be able to," was the only comment he was able to elicit on the matter, as her uncle obliged with a list of interesting venues. It was a bad day for the girl. As she performed her housekeeping duties she felt torn apart by her two handicaps, as she saw them, each of them designed to destroy her burgeoning relationship with this Australian. If he knew she was 'backward', he would certainly lose interest, and if he knew she was rich, he was bound to become too interested.

She was cleaning up after tea when he came back - straight into the kitchen. "Hello! You're home…" she said, her confused thoughts giving the words an uncertain tone. "Yes". He came towards her, taking a packet from his pocket. "I brought you a scarf - reckoned it would look good with your hair". He shook off the wrapping and held it out - a glowing green in what looked like finest silk. "Oh. It's lovely." She didn't know what to say and the gift made the situation worse. As she stood there, Mick unfolded the scarf and draped it round her shoulders. The he stepped back. "It's just as I thought," he said. "Makes you look pretty as a picture." At that moment Father Tom called out, "How did the day go? Did you see the Spanish Arch? Did you find Lynch's house?"

"Yes, I did". With a little smile, Mick turned and went to join the priest.

Celia ran upstairs and looked in the mirror. Yes, the scarf did suit her, made her look a different person, actually. But she couldn't wear it - it was leading him on - pretending she was normal, when… in despair, she wrenched it off.

She had to tell him, she decided eventually and, when her uncle had gone over to the church to hear confessions, she found him writing in the study. He got up as soon as she came in and put down his pen. "I didn't mean to upset you this morning." he said. "Is there something bad about Galway for you"?

"No". She was blurting it out. "It's that I can't write - I was no good at school - folk say I'm backward". There it was. Now he knew. He would be shocked…

But Mick took her hand and questioned her gently. After a while he began to laugh. "You're not backward, Celia. What you have is dyslexia. It's quite common - it doesn't mean you're stupid - you just can't get the right words down on paper."

Celia tried to take this in, as he continued to hold her hand. "I've a confession to make myself", he told her, after a few minutes. "I came over here because my father died and

I inherited the family ranch - oh - thousands of acres - but I needed a wife and I couldn't be sure if any Aussie girl would be marrying me or the ranch..."

He stopped short, as Celia in her turn began to laugh. But she had no time to tell him why before he pulled her towards him and silenced her laughter with a kiss.

THE SHOOTER

———

THINGS WERE GOING FROM BAD TO WORSE ALONG THE WESTERN SEABOARD IN THE LATE 1800S. RESENTMENT WAS BUILDING UP AMONG THE TENANTS AND THE LANDLORDS WERE ON EDGE, SUSPICIOUS OF EVERY MOVE AND EVICTING TENANTS ON THE LEAST PROVOCATION. A FENIAN UPRISING WAS IN THE OFFING AND EVIDENCE OF GUN-RUNNING HAD THE COAST GUARD ON FULL ALERT.

Squire Basil Randolph had the worst reputation thereabouts for oppression and evictions. His very appearance caused shudders of fright among all who were dependent upon him, he being extremely dark-haired and skinny with a hawk-like face and likened by many to the devil himself. His demesne, Drayton Hall, covered tracts of mountainous acres and reared vast flocks of sheep, which were tended by shepherds, who lived in isolated cabins. In some ways this isolation gave them a feeling of security, while in others it made them objects of suspicion. A family had recently been thrown out on the pretext of poaching and another had fallen foul of Randolph's agent, in an altercation over the price of oats.

The McGintys seemed set to be the next victims of Randolph's suspicion. Tomas and Bridget, with their young son Eoin, lived in the foothills above Lough Fionn. Several times in the last month the landlord's agent had ridden by the cabin, supposedly to check on the sheep, but more likely Tomas reckoned, to check on himself.

The last time was only two days ago and at his departure, Bridget had set up a wailing and crying that their time had come, that they were for the road, surely, themselves and the lad, headed for starvation, or the workhouse. He had tried to calm her, but could find no real words of comfort for what in his heart he knew to be true.

RAFTERS

So, desperate situations required desperate measures, and now he was reaching for the gun in the rafters as the thought spun around in his mind.

It was time to put a stop to the brutal reprisals on the part of the Squire against his tenants and he was not the only one, he was certain, who felt the same way. For a long time he had felt that the landlord, in particular, regarded him, with deep suspicion, due to the fact that his cousin, Danny Moran, had been arrested on a charge of arson on the neighbouring Balfour estate. Danny was a Fenian, and it was a Fenian gun that Tomas now lifted down and cradled in his arms.

He was not himself a member of any gang - in spite of the urging of his cousin and the disaffected tenants. He was more interested in the illicit still he had set up in the mountains for brewing the poteen that dulled the misery of their lot. But now, there was nothing to loose - eviction meant the end for the family and he was determined to get the swine of a landlord first.

He had sent his wife and the boy to the shebeen of Malachy Coyne to sell a few quarts of the hard stuff to get them out of the way and now it was time to move himself. Toting the gun, he stepped down off the chair and left the cabin.

He knew that on this day, the Squire would be riding into Drumlish to the house of his agent to assess the rental payments of his tenants. And he would pass along the Garvary boreen. At one point the boreen ran between two steep banks and it was from behind one of these that he planned to commit the dastardly deed.

It was now round four o'clock in the afternoon. Tomas kept to the heather-clad slopes that lay between him and his destination avoiding the stony path where someone might be encountered. His mind was totally focused on his forthcoming act; no thought of consequences entered it, he was simply fuelled by the over-powering sense of injustice, to the exclusion of all else.

At last, the trees which enclosed the section of the boreen he was aiming for, lay ahead. He proceeded furtively and surveyed the bank, below which lay the track. He finally selected the cover of a rhododendron bush growing at the top and crawled up to lie concealed among the leaves.

He was barely in position, when the clip clop of a horse's hooves announced the approach of his quarry. The Squire on his big bay stallion, rounded a corner and came briskly up the slight incline Tomas aimed the gun, his finger on the trigger.

A split second before he squeezed it, a jay flew screeching from the branches of a nearby oak, the stallion reared in fright and, as the shot rang out, its rider was thrown backwards onto the ground.

Simultaneously the horse bolted and a figure, also clutching a gun, toppled from the opposite bank to lie in the boreen beside the inert figure of the Squire, blood seeping from beneath his cap.

Tomas was frozen in place. Had he killed two people? Whose was the second body? He stared down at the scene of carnage. There was no movement, or sound - apart from the fading noise of the stallion's drumming hooves.

How long passed? He could never afterwards be sure but, almost in a daze, he eventually slid down the bank, still holding his gun, and bent over the bleeding man. He was dead, obviously. Shot through the head.

By himself? And what of the Squire? He turned towards his intended victim as Randolph stirred and raised his head, seeing the bearded, wild-looking face of his suspect tenant bending over him. "I knew it," he said. "Fenians - the whole clan. You have me at your mercy now, but make no mistake, you'll not escape the law!"

With a groan of pain, he lay back, while Tomas continued to dither indecisively beside him. One death on his hands was enough - there was no way that he could raise his gun and shoot a defenceless man point blank.

He returned his scrutiny to the dead body. It was no one he knew, although it was someone with the same end in view. And it could just as easily have been himself lying there, he realised, if the other's finger had been fractionally faster on the trigger.

As he gazed down at the lifeless figure, the Squire's voice broke into his thoughts. The landlord had revived and was also surveying the corpse. "By God, McGinty," he said, "I've done you an injustice. It appears that you've saved my life."

Tomas made no reply, although it seemed, in fact, true. He was thinking that if the law did not, after all, get him, the other tenants would.

Randolph laid a hand on his shoulder. "I'd be extremely grateful, my man," he said, "If you could assist me to get home. Alive I may be, but I fear, somewhat injured."

DAZE

It was still in a daze that Tomas found he was supporting his landlord and arranging the gun under his arm as a crutch, as he limped painfully back along the way that he had come. They had proceeded some distance when the stallion was spotted, grazing on a patch of grass, with trailing reins.

"Could you ride, sir, if I caught him?" asked Tomas. He had no wish to be seen in such close proximity to the enemy.

"I believe I could," was the reply, and he crept towards the animal and seized the bridle. After a startled plunge, he was able to lead it back and heave the injured man into the saddle. Once balanced, Randolph looked down. "Best give me the gun, McGinty," he said, "and I leave it to your discretion to dispose of the corpse."

Without demure, Tomas handed up the weapon, realising at the back of his mind that Randolph was protecting him. He said nothing, but stood back as horse and rider moved off slowly, then turned and hurried back to perform his gruesome work.

He dragged the body up the bank and down the other side. Beneath a fallen tree the upturned roots had formed a cavity and he concealed it there, scuffing dead leaves over it in addition, to prevent discovery until he was able to return with a spade and bury it. He kept the man's gun to replace his own… nothing was certain.

Back home, his wife and son had returned from the shebeen with the few shillings obtained for the poteen. His wife was gathering their meager possessions prior to expected eviction. "Any sign of thim devils along the road?" she asked Tomas anxiously as soon as he arrived.

He shook his head. "There is not," he told her, "I'm thinking, perhaps, they'll not be coming." How to tell her that the danger might have altogether passed? The truth must never out.

The woman muttered disbelievingly and made no move to put the things away. She asked no questions when he shouldered the slan next day and made off down the hillside, and he volunteered no explanation.

But there were anxious days ahead, she waited for the bailiffs to evict them, he for retribution for the killing. No sign of either came.

It was two months later when Randolph's agent came riding to McGinty's. Tomas heard the clatter of hooves on stone and his eyes went up to the rafters, but, "He is, you honour," he heard his wife's unsteady voice, and he went out to face disaster with defiance.

Against all expectations, it was not bad news the agent brought. "You are to be head shepherd," said the man. "Squire Randolph gives you tenure of Sloe Cottage in the Bracken Valley. Report to me for orders in two day's time." He threw a key down at Tomas' feet, turned his horse and rode away.

"In the name of God," said Bridget, blessing herself, "what has brought this to pass?"

"Tis just luck," replied her husband, but his own voice was unsteady with disbelief. "Now be gathering up our things again and we'll be away to Bracken Valley." They piled their worldly goods into the panniers on their donkey's back, prior to departure - all except the dead man's gun, which remained in the rafters to save the next tenant from eviction.

ASTRAY...IN THE HEAD

"And may the Lord give the Squire a change of heart."

"AMEN". THE FAMILY CROSSED THEMSELVES AND ROSE FROM THEIR KNEES AFTER HAVING RECITED THE ROSARY, KNOWING FULL WELL THAT SIR MERVYN ROSS HAD NO HEART IN HIM AND THEREFORE NOTHING COULD CHANGE. THIS TIME THE FOLLOWING DAY THEY WOULD BE OUT ON THEIR EARS AT THE SIDE OF THE ROAD WITH THE CABIN IN RUINS BEHIND THEM.

In an uneasy silence they huddled round the hearth - the elderly couple and their remaining son, eighteen-year-old Marty. The rush light guttered and spooky shadows made the dusk more menacing. Marty swayed back and forth on his stool, his red untidy hair falling into his eyes. Suddenly he was still, head on one side, listening. "I hear her!" he exclaimed. "She's calling me - I must go". He got up abruptly, overturning the stool, and made for the door.

His parents moved as if to restrain him, but he was out the door and away before a hand could be laid on him. "God help us", muttered his mother, "and him to be gone in our hour of need".

"Sure, what good is he?" retorted her spouse, Peader Gavin, "and he astray in the head. If he could do some work itself, the Sir might not be in such a hurry to evict us".

His wife moaned helplessly.

Meanwhile, in the fading light, Marty ran over the heather towards the cliffs. The distant sound of what some might have taken to be the wail of a banshee luring him on. He knew it for what it was, the selchie's call. The seal-woman had come for him. Since he had turned eighteen, he had been expecting it. Now they would go off together and live happily ever after.

The folk lore of Mayo abounded in tales of the seals. It was common knowledge that a seal could assume human form and take a lover from among men. Many times Marty had seen his bride-to-be on the rocks, singing to herself and waiting, waiting until he came of age.

And now the time had come! Excitement mounting, he reached the cliffs and peered out across the darkening waters. Some way from the shore was a rock that he had often sat on to observe the seals. When the tide came in, it was cut off and on high tides it disappeared completely beneath the waves.

The call of the selchie was coming from that rock.

Marty ran to where the land dipped and he could scramble down to the shore. The moon was beginning to rise and it cast a faint silver path towards the rock. He never hesitated, but plunged into the water. With powerful strokes he set out, as confident in the sea himself as a seal.

The high-pitched calling continued and as he drew nearer it seemed to alternate with the sound of sobbing. She thinks I'm not heeding her, he concluded and redoubled his efforts to reach the rendezvous. He raised his head and, sure enough, a form was lying on the rock.

His feet grounded on a ledge and he pulled himself up to the flat surface above. Then he gasped and was rooted to the spot by what he saw.

It was not a beautiful selchie maiden, but a little boy, who was now crawling towards him and crying piteously. Just beyond, a dark body slithered into the sea and disappeared. Completely baffled and unable to relate the scene to anything he had expected, Marty just gazed uncomprehendingly at the boy, who approached him now crying "Papa, papa". Still he made no move, but the child made to climb on his back. "Take me home", he wailed. "I want Papa'.

The realization that his seal-woman had not come to meet him finally dawned on the frustrated young man. Instead, here was a castaway, crying for help. He pushed the child up on his back and the terrified boy wrapped his arms and legs around him, as he returned to the water and headed for the shore.

"Home. I want to go home", wailed the child, as Marty stumbled onto the beach. The castaway was stuck to his back like a limpet, there was no dislodging.

"Home - yes". That was where Marty intended to go and he set off at speed, up the rocky incline and along the edge of the cliffs, the moon now bright in the sky.

Back at the cabin his parents were still round the fire, too agitated to think of sleep. When Marty and his strange burden burst in the door, they stood up gasping. "Mother of God!' exclaimed his mother. "What have you got there?"

"It's a castaway", replied her son. "The selchie was calling me to the rock and I found him there. Could it be a seal-boy?" At this thought he reached round and with difficulty detached his rider and gazed at him. "I want to go home", wailed the boy again, as he was landed, dripping and shivering on the floor.

"You are home", Marty told him.

"Let you be quiet". Peadar pushed forward and examined the newcomer. "Tell us your name, boy", he said gently, after taking in the good quality of the drenched garments.

"I'm Bobby", came the sobbing answer.

"Bobby who?"

"Bobby…"

"Come to the fire, a gradh, and after a while you can tell us where you live". Bridget Gavin shoved the men aside and drew the boy to her. She stripped off his clothes and wrapped him in a flannel petticoat, she pulled from behind her chair. "Get a sup of milk for him", she commanded, as she soothed and petted him. Peadar warmed a cupful and the child sipped it with wide eyes, that were fixed all the time on Marty. Finally he held out his arms to his rescuer. "Seal-man", he murmured, seemingly caught up in the seal fantasy himself. Marty, now in dry clothes, took a hold of him, lay down on the rough straw mattress and both of them were soon sleeping.

Peadar and Bridget stared at each other. "This is a fine mess", said the former. "Us for the road tomorrow and now a child thrust upon us!" What's to do, at all, when a ditch is likely to be all we'll have to shelter us?"

"God is good", muttered his wife. "With his help the bailiffs will leave us in peace".

But neither of them believed that and they dozed off by the fire, ready in their hearts to face destitution and the work house.

Morning came and all were awake early. There was a pot of stirabout to be warmed up and the little boy was coaxed to eat some. Then Bridget dressed him in his dried clothes. "We should take him home", she said.

"And how can we do that', demanded her husband, "when we don't know where it is? And how can we leave here, when the devil's henchmen are expected?

Bridget smoothed the little lad's jumper and tied the laces on his shoes. "Where is your own house, lovey?" she asked, when she was satisfied with is appearance.

"On the hill", said Bobby. "Far away".

Peadar shook his head. "Could be anywhere. But how did he get on the rock", he looked at his son, "if what that omadán says is true?"

The omadan in question was whittling a piece of driftwood with a knife, watched attentively by Bobby. Soon the child uttered a cry of delight. "It's a seal! Make him sitting on the rock". Marty duly obliged and eventually an exquisite carving of one of the sleek animals lying on the rock, it's head raised in calling, emerged from the raw material. Delight at this gift kept the little boy quiet until well into the morning, when a shout from Peadar brought everyone outside. In the distance could be seen a group of men following a horse and cart and headed by a mounted rider.

Bridget crossed herself. "Who are they?" Bobby wanted to know.

"Bad men", Bridget told him, "coming to knock down our house". She pulled him back inside, followed by the two men, who shut the door. Then they all stood waiting tremulously for what was to come. The child started to cry.

The rumble of the cart got louder. Then it stopped. There was the sound of pulling and hauling, a heavy thud and raised voices. Then a shouted command, "Come out of there and be on your way before the house is knocked!"

Peadar opened the door and they edged out, clutching their pathetic bundles of possessions. The man on the horse was recognizable as Sir Mervyn's land agent. The others were manhandling the tree trunk to be used as a battering ram. "Come on, come one, stand aside there!" came the impatient order and the little group shuffled sideways, leaving Bobby momentarily exposed in front.

The agent gave an audible gasp and reined back his horse. "God's truth!" He exclaimed. "It's master Bobby! And the troops out scouring the country for you".

He slid off the horse. "Come on 'till I take you home without delay". He approached the child, who screamed, "Bad man", and ran behind Marty, clutching his legs. The young man picked him up.

The agent was baffled. Then he hastily remounted. "I'll inform his Lordship", he said and called over his shoulder as he turned, "Don't touch the house meanwhile".

Dazed now themselves at the turn of events, but thankful for the respite, the family went back inside the cabin. An uneasy hour passed by, during which Bobby resumed his limpet-like grip on Marty's back. A clatter of hooves announced the arrival of the Lord and his agent. This time there was a knock at the door. "Is Bobby there?" asked an aloof English voice.

"Papa!" from Bobby, as Peadar opened the door to reveal the inmates and the callers to each other.

"Please explain how you have my son", said Lord Ross. "He simply disappeared from the garden of the house, where he was playing, last night".

"I heard the seal, Papa", said the boy from his safe perch. "The seal Nanny told me of. He called me and I went to the rock and the water came up and I couldn't leave. But the seal stayed with me and sang and then the seal-man came and saved me."

"Is this true?" His father looked at Peadar.

"So Marty says, your Honour", answered Peadar. "It would seem to be so, but my son is astray in the head and we cannot always be sure".

"I am in your debt. If it's true, my son could have drowned". Lord Ross put a handful of coins on the rough table. "Come, then, Bobby".

"I'm coming on the seal-man", said the child. He urged the bewildered Marty outside. Then his father saw the carving of a seal he was clutching.

"What's that you're holding?" he asked.

"It's my seal", said the boy. "The man made if for me".

Sir Mervyn examined it. "This is a work of art", he said. And turning back, "If your boy made this, he is not astray in the head, but a genius. If he comes to the hall, I'll provide him with a workshop and every facility".

"Sir", said Bridget, "it's the will of God, surely. And our house…?"

"Remain in peace", was the answer and a gesture was made to the waiting agent, who in turn ordered his crew to pack up and leave.

The man and woman watched the departure, watched their despaired-of-son walk off to a new life, carrying the Ross's heir and - although of course they didn't know it at the time - to become a wood carver of national renown, who would bring them great comfort in their declining years.

THE STONES OF RUSHEEN

ANDY, THE SHEPHERD, CAME OVER THE HILL FROM CARROWMORE AS THE FIRST WISPS OF SMOKE WERE RISING FROM THE CABINS IN THE VALLEY. HE MADE HIS WAY DOWN THE ROCKY SLOPE UNTIL HE STOOD WITHOUT THE FIRST OF THE RAGGED LINE OF DWELLINGS. 'COME OUT, OWEN DUBH'! HE SHOUTED. 'MAY YOUR NEXT SLEEP BE AS PEACEFUL'!

In a moment the top half of the door swung back and the black-bearded face of Owen Gowlan was framed in the opening. 'What's this to do'? he growled. 'Have you lost your wits, or what'?

'My wits are not lost', retorted the shepherd. But your house will likely be lost the morrow'.

'What's that you're saying'? Owen opened the bottom half of the door and emerged to confront the old man.

'I'm telling you that Squire Brodie is on the rampage, that four families were evicted yesterday from Carrowmore and the word is that you're next on the list'.

'Oh, the Lord save us'! A wail went up from inside the cottage and the inmates crowded in confusion in the doorway - Bridget, the woman of the house, the two young sons, Kitty, the seventeen-year-old and Owen's aged mother, Martha, who continued to wail and beseech the Lord for assistance.

Owen himself, momentarily silenced from shock, soon found his voice again. 'Bad cess to him' he roared. 'I'll not be bested by that divil's whelp!

'You'll be hard put to best the likes of him', replied Andy, 'with his team of wreckers and their big battering ram to stave in the doors'!

'Stave in the door, is it'? Owen was stamping with rage. 'Well, that's the last thing he'll do'! He turned back to his family. 'To work, the lot of ye'! He shouted. 'Gather up the biggest stones you can find and bring them here to me'.

'The Lord have mercy on us'! A renewed wail from the old woman, who retreated back to the hearth, exempt by her age from the task ahead.

'Good luck to ye, then', and the shepherd was away, leaving a scene of commotion behind him. It was not easy to find the stones Owen demanded. Walls were tumbled and hands were bruised and bleeding as they lugged and heaved, piling up the acceptable material inside the cabin.

'Stones, stones', moaned old Martha. 'It's not these stones will save us. If I was in my health, I'd be off to the stones of Rusheen, and they'd do a job on the Squire, I'm telling you'.

'Ah, be quiet, Mam' Owen had overheard her as he had come in with a big flag. 'It's time those old superstitions were forgot'.

Kitty, too, had overheard her Grandmother and, red curls blown into a tangle about her face, was glad of an excuse to rest from the labour and sat down beside her. 'What stones are those, then, Nan', she asked. 'Where are the stones that might help us'?

'They're at the point of Rusheen, child. That's where they are.' Martha was delighted to have a listener. 'They're laid out on an altar at the top of the cliff - seven stones, each in its hollow. The cursing stones'.

'How do they work'? Kitty desired only to prolong her rest.

'You turn each one of them', the old woman continued, 'and as you turn it, always going against the clock, you call down the curse. It's great power that does be in them. . . '

'Come on. Work's not over yet'! Her father's voice brought the girl to her feet again and she returned to the task until Bridget called a halt for a dinner of stew and yellow meal bread.

Eventually Owen declared that they had enough stones gathered and he ordered them all inside. 'Now', he told them, 'We're going to build a wall at the back of the door that will defy them varmints to break it down'. The old woman mumbled and Bridget put her arms around the boys, while hopeless tears ran down her cheeks.

'I'll stay outside, Dad', Kitty suddenly spoke up. 'Someone needs to see to the cow and to let ye know what's happening. 'I can sleep with Kirwins beyond,' she finished.

'You're right, lass', her father agreed after some thought. 'But don't be sighted by the squireen'.

'I'll take good care', and Kitty slipped out before the door was closed and the building inside begun.

All the afternoon her grandmother's words, 'the stones of Rusheen', had been repeating in her mind. She wondered if the story of the curse could be true. Gradually she made the decision that it was worth a try. The situation was desperate and if harm should befall Squire Brodie, she knew that his son did not hold with evicting the tenants. As evening was falling she set out for the coast. She had never been that far, but she had heard tell of Rusheen point - the nearest part of the country to America, as was said. It should be easy to find.

Night fell, but darkness was not complete and after a while the moon shone out and was suddenly sparkling silver on the sea before her as she breasted a low hill. She turned south, a prayer in her heart that she would find the place.

And she did. Rusheen point was unmistakeable - big cliffs jutting out into the sea with the land falling away behind. Tentatively making her way along the top of the promintary, she had almost reached the outermost edge when she came upon the altar - a slightly-raised slab of rock with seven white stones nestled around the center in hollow cups.

Taking a death breath, Kitty grasped the first stone and began twisting it from right to left. 'May the devil take Squire Brodie and prevent him from evicting us', she muttered, going from stone to stone, anti-clock-wise and repeating the words each time, as Martha had described.

When she had completed the circuit, she felt completely drained of energy and, after crawling back to a safer position, she stretched out on the rough sward and fell instantly asleep.

The moonlight was fading when she woke with a gasp. What had come over her, she did not know and anxiety flooded her thoughts. What if the evil posse arrived before she could warn the family? Getting to her feet, she began to run; stumbling at first over the bumps and hummocks of the untilled land, she soon lengthened her stride and moved rapidly back along the way she had come and dawn was lighting her path as she picked her way across the valley bottom and scrambled up the rise below the cabin.

A nightmare scene confronted her: before the cabin door six men wielded a tree trunk, preparatory to ramming it forward. Just to the side a rider on a big black horse watched the proceedings.

As the team drew backwards to launch the blow on the door, Kitty let out a piercing scream and then everything happened so quickly that she was scarcely able to take it in. Startled by her scream, the black horse reared up and threw its rider behind the team of men as they launched their forward rush. When the tree trunk hit the door, instead of splintering all before it, the solid barrier it encountered caused it to spring backwards just as the fallen rider raised up his head from the ground. With a blow that would have felled an ox, the missile struck.

Squire Reginald Brodie breathed his last on the threshold of the only cabin that had ever resisted his evil onslaught.

Many's the bonfire that burned the following night in Carrowmore and in the Annagh valley. Owen Dubh was hailed as a hero and his strategy with the built up doorway was written into local folk lore.

As for Kitty - she had not been missed and she never breathed a word about her escapade. Who would credit the stones of Rusheen with the squireen's death, when all and sundry knew that it was her father, Black Owen Gowan, who had defeated the enemy? But a big laugh rose inside her when, chortling by the fire, old Martha told whoever was listening that 'Someone surely turned the stones of Rusheen on our behalf this day'.

ABOUT THE AUTHOR

———

Feature writer for many years for the Irish Press and the Irish Farmer's Journal. Book on the Connemara pony published by the Mercier Press. Have written short stories for the radio and for various newspapers and magazines, including Ireland's Own and Ireland's Eye. Currently have a broadcasting slot on a local radio station and write a column for a local newspaper. Married into an island family off the west coast of Ireland and thus heard many tales of the hardship endured by the native people during the previous centuries, and also of their exploits and derring-do. This gave me an insight into their thinking and way of speaking, which I have tried to echo in these stories.

Printed in the United Kingdom
by Lightning Source UK Ltd.
112039UKS00001B/112-264